Gregory Mcdonald

Fletch

Gregory Mcdonald is the author of twenty-five books, including nine Fletch novels and three Flynn mysteries. He has twice won the Mystery Writers of America's prestigious Edgar Allan Poe Award for Best Mystery Novel, and was the first author to win for both a novel and its sequel. He lives in Tennessee.

Books by Gregory Mcdonald

Gregory Mcdonald

Fletch

Vintage Crime/Black Lizard
Vintage Books
A Division of Random House, Inc.
New York

FIRST VINTAGE CRIME/BLACK LIZARD EDITION, MARCH 2002

The Cataloging-in-Publication Data is on file in the Library of
Congress.

Vintage ISBN: 0-375-71354-9

www.vintagebooks.com

Printed in the United States of America
10   9   8   7   6   5   4   3   2   1

To Susie, Judy and Lew Clapp

Fletch

1

"What's your name?"

"Fletch."

"What's your full name?"

"Fletcher."

"What's your first name?"

"Irwin."

"What?"

"Irwin. Irwin Fletcher. People call me Fletch."

"Irwin Fletcher, I have a proposition to make to you. I will give you a thousand dollars for just listening to it. If you decide to reject the proposition, you take the thousand dollars, go away, and never tell anyone we talked. Fair enough?"

"Is it criminal? I mean, what you want me to do?"

"Of course."

"Fair enough. For a thousand bucks I can listen. What do you want me to do?"

"I want you to murder me."

The black shoes tainted with sand came across the oriental rug. The man took an envelope from an inside pocket of his suit jacket and dropped it into Fletch's lap. Inside were ten one-hundred-dollar bills.

The man had returned the second day to the sea wall to watch Fletch. Only thirty yards away, he used binoculars.

The third day, he met Fletch at the beer stand.

"I want you to come with me."

"Why?"

"I want to make you an offer."

"I'm not that way."

"Neither am I. There's a job I might like to have you do for me."

"Why can't we talk here?"

"This is a very special job."

"Where are we going?"

"To my house. I'll want you to know where it is. Do you have any clothes on the beach?"

"Just a shirt."

"Get it. My car is a gray Jaguar XKE, parked at the curb. I will be waiting in it for you."

"I want to drink my beer first."

"Bring it with you. You can drink it in the car."

Walking away through the beach crowd, the man looked as out of place in his dark business suit as an insurance adjuster at a jalopy jamboree. No one appeared to notice him.

Keeping his shirt over it, Fletch picked up the plastic bag off the sand.

He sat a few feet away from his group, his shirt over the plastic bag beside him. Looking at the ocean, he drank some of the beer he held in his left hand. With his right hand he dug a hole in the sand under his shirt.

"What's happening?" Bobbi asked.

She was belly-down on a towel.

"Thinkin'."

He put the plastic bag into the hole and covered it over with sand.

"I guess I'm splittin'," he said. "For a while."

"Will you be back tonight?"

"I dunno."

Slinging his shirt over his shoulder, he started away.

"Gimme a swallow before you go."

Bobbi jacked herself on her elbow and took some of the beer.

"That's good," she said.

"Hey, man," Creasey said.

2

Fletch said, "Splittin'. Too much sun."

The license plate of the car was 440-001.

In the car, Fletch sat with the can of cold beer between his knees. The man drove smoothly and silently. Below sunglasses, the man's face was expressionless. On his left hand was a college ring. He used a gold cigarette lighter from his jacket pocket rather than the dashboard lighter.

In the shorefront traffic, the air-conditioner was making the car cold. Fletch opened the window. The man turned the air-conditioner off.

He took the main road going north from town and accelerated. The car cornered beautifully on the curves going up into The Hills. He slowed, turned left on Hawthorne, then right on Berman Street.

The house was what made Berman Street a dead end. If it weren't for signs on the iron-grilled gate saying PRIVATE PROPERTY—NO TRESPASSING—STANWYK, the road would appear to continue straight onto the driveway. There were two acres of lawn on each side of the driveway in front of the house.

Fletch threw his beer can through the window onto the lawn. The man did not appear to notice.

The house was built like a Southern mansion, with white pillars before a deep verandah.

The man closed the door to the library behind them.

"Why do you want to die?"

The envelope weighed little in the palm of Fletch's right hand.

"I am facing a long, ugly, painful and certain death."

"How so?"

"A while ago I was told I have cancer. I've had it checked and had it rechecked. It's terminal. Nonoperable, nontreatable cancer."

"You don't look it."

"I don't feel it. A kind of general rottenness. It's in its early stages. The docs say it will be a while before it's noticeable to others. Then it will move very swiftly."

"How long will it take?"

"They say three months, maybe four. Not six months, anyway. From what they say, I would guess in a month from now I won't be able to conceal that I have it."

"So? A month's a month."

"When you make a decision like this . . . that you're going . . . to be dead . . . you uh . . . decide to do it as quickly, as soon as possible. You try to cut the dying time."

Hands behind his back, the man was facing the french windows. Fletch guessed he was in his early thirties.

"Why don't you kill yourself? Why do you need me?"

"My company has me insured for three million dollars. I have a wife and child. There is no point in losing the money, which I would, or rather my heirs would, if I committed suicide. On the other hand, for three million dollars it's not worth going through that much pain and unpleasantness. I believe I have made an entirely rational decision."

The paintings in the room were not particularly good, in Fletch's opinion, but they were real.

"Why me?"

"You're a drifter. You suddenly showed up in town. You just as suddenly leave. No one will think about it in particular, or connect you with the murder. There will be no way of connecting you and me. You see, I have planned your escape. It is very important to me that you escape. If you were caught, and talked, as you would, the insurance would be voided."

"Supposing I'm not a drifter. Supposing I'm just on vacation."

"Is that what you're telling me? That you're on vacation?"

"No."

"I've been watching you off and on the last few days. You're on the beach with the dregs of society. You associate exclusively with drug addicts. I must assume you are one yourself."

"Maybe I'm a cop."

"Are you?"

"No."

"You have a deep body tan, Irwin Fletcher. You're as skinny as an alley cat. The soles of your feet are callused. You've been on the road a long time."

4

"Why did you pick me over the other kids on the beach?"

"You're no kid. You look younger, but you're almost thirty."

"I'm twenty-nine."

"You're not as far gone as the others. You're addicted, I suppose. Otherwise you couldn't stand to live with those freaks. But you still seem able to operate."

"I'm a fairly reliable-looking drifter."

"Don't feel complimented."

Fletch said, "What makes you think I want to commit murder?"

"Twenty thousand dollars. And a guarantee you won't get caught."

After staring out the window, it took the man's eyes a moment to adjust to the room. He was unable to look at Fletch without an expression of mild disgust.

"You can't tell me you don't need money. Addicts always need money. Even beginners. Maybe your taking this opportunity will prevent your committing more genuine crimes."

"Why isn't this a genuine crime?"

"It's a mercy killing. Are you married?"

"I have been," Fletch said. "Twice."

"And now you're on the road. From where are you originally?"

"Seattle."

"So you commit an act of mercy, make some money, and split. What's wrong with that?"

"I don't know. I'm not sure."

"Are you ready for more?"

"More what?"

"More of the plan. Or are you ready to quit?"

"I'm ready. Go ahead."

"I want to die next Thursday, a week from tonight, at about eight-thirty. It should look like the usual murder-robbery scene. The servants will be out, as they are now, and my wife will be at a committee meeting at the Racquets Club.

"These french windows will be unlocked. The damned servants always forget to lock them anyway." He swung the door open and closed it with his hand. "I used to complain about it until I realized their stupidity could be useful. At the moment, we do not have a dog.

"I'll be in this room alone, waiting for you. I will already have opened the safe, and in it will be twenty thousand dollars, in tens and twenties, which will be yours after you have murdered me. I don't imagine opening a safe is one of your skills?"

"No."

"Too bad. It would look better if it were authentically burglarized. At least be sure to wear gloves. I don't want you to get caught.

"In the drawer here," he said, reaching inside the top right-hand desk drawer, "is a gun which is always loaded." It was a .38 caliber Smith & Wesson. The man showed him that it was loaded. "I figure you should use my gun, so no one can trace it to you. Before you come, I will mess up the house a bit to indicate robbery.

"The trick will be to make it look as if I have caught you at burglary, you have already been in my desk, you have my gun, you shoot me. Can you shoot?"

"Yes."

"Were you in the service?"

"Yes. Marines."

"Either the head or the heart. Just make it quick and painless, and, for Christ's sake, make sure you're thorough. Do you have a passport?"

"No," Fletch lied.

"Of course not. Get one. That should be the first order of business, as that will take time. It's not tourist season, so it shouldn't take more than three or four days. But get started tomorrow.

"After you murder me, you will drive the Jaguar, which will be parked out front, to the airport. Leave the car in the Trans World Airlines parking lot. You will be taking the eleven o'clock flight to Buenos Aires. I will make the reservation, and pay for it, in your name, tomorrow. I figure twenty thousand dollars should buy you some fun in Buenos Aires. For a year or two."

"Fifty thousand dollars would buy me even more fun."

"You want fifty thousand dollars? Murder doesn't cost that much."

"You forget you're to be the victim. You want it done humanely."

The man's eyes narrowed contemptuously.

"You're right. Of course. I guess fifty thousand dollars can be arranged without causing suspicion."

The man returned to stare through the french windows. Clearly he did not like looking at Fletch.

"I'm doing everything I can to guarantee that you don't get caught. All you have to remember are gloves and a passport. The gun will be provided, and a seat on the plane will be reserved and pre-paid."

The man asked, "Will you murder me?"

Fletch said, "Sure."

2

"Clara?"

"Where are you, Fletcher?"

"I'm in a phone booth."

"Are you all right?"

"Sure."

"I was afraid of that."

"I love you, too, bitch."

"Endearments will get you nowhere."

"There's nowhere I want to get with you. Listen: I'm driving up tonight."

"To the office?"

"Yes."

"Why?"

"I think I'm onto something interesting."

"Does it have to do with the drugs-on-the-beach story?"

"As a matter of fact, no."

"Then I don't want to hear about it."

"I'm not going to tell you about it anyway."

"Frank was asking for the drug-beach story again this afternoon."

"Fuck Frank."

"He wants it, Fletcher. That's scheduled as a major magazine story, and you were supposed to be in with it three issues ago."

"I'm doing fine with it."

"He wants it now, Fletcher. With pictures. Frank was pretty boiled this afternoon, and you know how much I love you."

"You'd stick up for me, wouldn't you, Clara?"

"In a pig's ass."

"You can't take me off the story now, and Frank knows it. I've got too much time in on it. Besides, no one else in the office has my tan."

"What we can do is fire you for failure to complete an assignment."

"Why don't you stop talking, Clara? I said I'm driving up tonight."

"There are some people who are just too goddamned obnoxious to have around."

"Meaning me?"

"Which reminds me, Fletcher. Another sleazy lawyer was around the office again this afternoon looking for you. Something about nonpayment of alimony."

"Which wife this time?"

"How the hell do I know? Don't you pay either of them?"

"They both wanted to be free of me. They're both free."

"But the court says you're not free of them."

"When I want legal advice, Clara, I'll ask."

"Keep those bums out of the office. Your alimony problems are not our problems."

"Right, Clara."

"And don't come back here until you have that goddamned story done."

"I can miss a day with the little darlings. I sort of told the kids I was splitting anyway. For a while. I can get back here by tomorrow night. And have another wonderful weekend on the beach."

"I said no, Fletcher. If you've accomplished anything at all down there, you must have caused some curiosity. Going for your car now and driving up to the office would just expose everything. You shouldn't even be in a phone booth talking to me."

"I want to come up to make some phone calls and do some digging."

"On this story? The beach one?"

"No. The other one."

"We don't give a damn about any other story until you finish this one."

"Clara? I'm cold. I'm still in swimming trunks."

"I care. Get off the phone and get doin' what you're supposed to be doin'. It's seven-thirty, and I've had a long day."

"Bye, Clara. Nice talking with you. Don't get any crumbs in Frank's bed."

"Prick."

Running on the beach warmed him. The setting sun made his shadow gigantic, his strides seem enormous. There were people still on the beach, as there always were these days. Taking off his shirt as he ran made his shadow on the sand look as if he were Big Bird trying to take off.

Near Fat Sam's lean-to, he threw his shirt on the sand and sat beside it. His aim had been perfect. Under the shirt he dug up the plastic bag. His fingers told him that the camera was still inside.

With the bag wrapped in his shirt, Fletch ambled back along the beach to the residential section. The houses became more spacious and the distances between them greater.

A checkbook was on the sand. Fletch picked it up. *Merchants Bank.* No depositor's name was printed on the checks, but there was an account number, and a balance of seven hundred eighty-five dollars and thirty-four cents.

Fletch stuck the checkbook into a back pocket of his sawed-off blue jeans.

A man stoking a barbecue pit yelled at him as he cut through a back yard. Fletch gestured at him in Italian.

He picked up his keys in the office and padded over the grease-packed garage floor to where his MG was parked. In the trunk were long jeans and a sweater.

"Hey, jerk!" The guy in the office was fat and bald. "You can't change your pants in here. You can't strip in a public place."

9

"I did."

"Wise ass. What if some ladies were around?"

"There are no ladies in California."

He flicked on the tape recorder before he left the garage. The safety belt strapped the big tape recorder to the passenger seat. He had put the camera in the glove compartment.

The wire was draped around his neck. The microphone dangled beneath his chin.

"Alan Stanwyk," he said, waving as he passed the man still shouting at him from the office, "after keeping me under surveillance a few days while I have been investigating the source of drugs in The Beach area for the *News-Tribune,* has just commissioned me to murder him in exactly one week—next Thursday night at eight-thirty. His surveillance convinced him that I am in fact a drifter and a drug addict.

"At least I *think* it is Alan Stanwyk who has commissioned me to murder him. I had never seen Alan Stanwyk before, but the man who commissioned me to murder him brought me to the Stanwyk residence on Berman Street, The Hills. I know there is such a person as Alan Stanwyk—as Amelia Shurcliffe of the *News-Tribune* doubtlessly has referred to him a thousand times: Alan Stanwyk, the wealthy young socialite.

"A quick check of the picture files at the office will establish whether or not the man who commissioned me to murder him is in fact Alan Stanwyk.

"I must follow the journalistic instinct of being skeptical of everything until I personally have proved it true.

"Stanwyk's justification for this unique request, that I murder him, is that he is dying of cancer. I am without any diagnostic training, but I must say that to a layman's eye he looks a well and fit man.

"On the other hand, his manner is totally convincing.

"Further justification for the request is that his life is insured for three million dollars. Direct and obvious suicide on his part would nullify the insurance.

"The man who says he is Stanwyk says he has a wife and child.

"The plan he has worked out for his murder is detailed.

10

"Having a passport, I am to enter the Stanwyk house through the french windows in the library next Thursday evening at eight-thirty. His wife will be at a committee meeting at the Racquets Club. The servants will be gone.

"Stanwyk will have arranged the house to make it appear a robbery has been committed. He will have opened the safe.

"I am to take a .38 caliber Smith & Wesson from the top right-hand drawer of the desk in the library and shoot Stanwyk to kill him, as painlessly as possible. He has shown me that the gun is loaded.

"I am then to drive his car, a gray Jaguar XKE, license number 440-001, to the airport and board the TWA eleven o'clock flight to Buenos Aires. A reservation in my name for that flight will be made tomorrow.

"For this service to Stanwyk, he has agreed to pay me fifty thousand dollars. He will have the cash in the house, in the opened safe, in tens and twenties when I arrive next week.

"Originally, he offered twenty thousand dollars. I pressed the price to fifty thousand dollars, in an effort to gauge his seriousness.

"He appeared serious.

"His investigation of me he believes to have been adequate. He watched me a few days and saw precisely that image I had been assigned to project: that of a drifter and a drug addict.

"He did not know my name or anything else about me.

"What Stanwyk doesn't realize is that I am the great hotshot young reporter, I.M. Fletcher of the *News-Tribune,* who so dislikes his first names, Irwin Maurice, that he never signs them. I am I.M. Fletcher. Down at The Beach trying to break a drug story.

"The questions at this point appear obvious enough.

"Is the man who commissioned me to murder him Alan Stanwyk?

"Does he have terminal cancer?

"Is he insured for three million dollars?

"Does he really mean for me to murder him?

"In the answer to any one of these questions, there is probably a helluva story.

"And although I admit to having been in the killing business for a while, in Indochina, I am now back in the helluva story business.

"Any story concerning Alan Stanwyk is worth getting.

"Therefore, I have agreed to murder Alan Stanwyk.

"My agreeing to murder him gives me exactly a week, in which I can be fairly sure he will not commission anyone else to murder him.

"Dishonest of me, I know.

"But as Pappy used to say about violating virgins, 'Son, if you're not the first, someone else will be.' "

3

"Carradine."

"This is I.M. Fletcher."

"Yes, Mr. Fletcher."

"I write for the *News-Tribune*."

"Oh."

"You are the financial editor, aren't you?"

"Are you that shit who wrote that piece saying we are headed for a moneyless state?"

"I did write something of the sort, yes."

"You're a shit."

"Thanks for buying the Sunday paper."

"I didn't. I read it Monday in the office."

"You see?"

"What can I do for you, Fletcher?"

A head peered through the door of Fletch's cubicle and smiled victoriously. The head was about forty years old, male, with bleached blond hair. Seeing Fletch on the telephone, it withdrew.

"I need some information about a man named Stanwyk. W-Y-K."

"*Alan* Stanwyk?"

"Yes."

The picture file on Fletch's desk was clearly of the man he had met yesterday. Alan Stanwyk in business suit, Alan Stanwyk in black tie, Alan Stanwyk in flight gear: Alan Stanwyk who wished to end his life—a murder mystery.

"He married Collins Aviation."

"All of it?"

"He married the only daughter of the president and chairman of the board."

"Job security."

"You should be so lucky."

"Frank, our supreme boss, doesn't have any daughters. Just sons of bitches."

"I believe Stanwyk is executive vice president of Collins Aviation."

"Will wonders never cease."

"I believe he's due to be president, once he gets a little more age on him."

"His future was made with the bed."

"No, I understand he's a competent fellow in his own right. Graduated from Harvard or Wharton—one of those places. A bright fellow who, as far as I know, is a perfectly nice man."

"How is Collins Aviation doing?"

"Very well, as far as I know. He runs the place. His father-in-law is virtually retired. Spends all his time running tournaments at the Racquets Club down at The Beach. And paying for them. The stock is solid. I don't know. I'd really have to look into it more. It's not a very active stock. It is publicly traded, but mostly it's held by Collins and a few of his cronies who are directors."

"So anything could be true, eh?"

"Almost anything. Do you want me to look further into this?"

"Yes."

"What do you need to know?"

"Everything. I want to know everything about Stanwyk, his wife, Collins, Collins Aviation, personal and professional."

"Why the Christ should I do your work for you?"

"You're the financial editor of the *News-Tribune*, aren't you?"

"Yes."

"I'd hate to make a mistake and have it reflect on you."

"Me? How could it reflect on me?"

"I've talked with you already."

"Clara Snow said you're a shit."

"My extension is 705. Many thanks."

"Christ."

"No. I.M. Fletcher."

The telephone book was stuffed into the bookcase behind his desk. While he was pulling it out, ignoring the papers that spilled on the floor from above and below the telephone book, the man who was not blond came in and sat down in Fletch's side chair.

"Mr. Fletcher?"

The man wore an open shirt and love beads.

"Yes."

"I'm Gillett, of Gillett, Worsham and O'Brien."

"No foolin'."

"Your wife's attorneys."

"Which wife?"

"Mrs. Linda Fletcher, as she is now known."

"Oh, really? Linda. How is she doin'?"

"Not well, Mr. Fletcher. Not well at all."

"I'm sorry to hear that. She's a nice kid."

"She is very distressed that since the divorce you have not paid her one cent in alimony."

"I took her to lunch once."

"She has told me about the King-size Relish Burger several times now. Your generosity has been marked. The alimony you owe her is three thousand, four hundred and twenty-nine dollars. Because of your generosity regarding the King-size Relish Burger, the few odd cents can be forgotten."

"Thanks."

COLLINS AVIATION: 553-0477.

"Tell me something, Mr. Worsham—"

"Gillett."

"As an attorney, I mean."

"I would not be allowed to have you as a client. I might add that I would not want you as a client."

"Nevertheless, there you are, sitting in a chair in my office, determined not to be thrown out, while I'm trying to get some work done. I know you come from a very distinguished law firm. Only partners of the most distinguished law firms come out personally to collect bills for three thousand dollars. You've been hanging around all week. It must be that your own office rent isn't paid. Or are you nicking Linda for more than three hundred of the three thousand?"

"What is your question, Mr. Fletcher?"

"As an attorney, Mr. Gillett, do you think it makes any difference that I never agreed to any alimony settlement? I have never even agreed to the divorce."

"I have nothing to do with that now. The court decided that you shall pay, and you shall."

"I mean, doesn't it strike you as peculiar that I came home one night and Linda wasn't there and the next thing I know I'm divorced for abandoning her?"

"This is not the first time this has happened to you, Mr. Fletcher. For a boy in your early or mid-twenties, two divorces on your record seem more than adequate."

"I'm sentimental. I keep believing in the old institutions."

"As long as you keep getting married . . ."

"I promise. I won't get married anymore. Being abandoned is too expensive."

"Mr. Fletcher. Mrs. Fletcher has told me a great deal about you."

"Did you ever buy her a King-size Relish Burger?"

"We've talked in my office."

"I thought so."

"She has told me that you are a vicious, violent man, a liar and a cheat, and that she left your bed and board because she absolutely couldn't stand you anymore. She did not abandon you. She escaped with her life."

"Vicious and violent. Bullshit. One night I stepped on the cat's tail."

"You pitched the cat through the window of your seventh-floor apartment."

"The whole place smelled of cat."

"Mrs. Fletcher, thinking reasonably that she might be the next one to go through the window, packed and left the very next time you left the apartment to go to work."

15

"Nonsense. She didn't smell. She was always in the shower. She washed her hair every half hour."

"Mr. Fletcher, as you have pointed out, I have been looking for you all week. For some reason, your office would not let me know where you were. I have the choice of bringing you back to court, and this time, I assure you, you will appear. Now, do you wish to arrange to make this payment here and now, or do you force me to go back to court?"

"Easier done than said." From his desk drawer Fletch took the checkbook he had found on the beach. The Merchants Bank. "It just so happens, Mr. Gillett, that I've been playing poker all week. I won seven thousand dollars. That's why my office didn't know where I was, of course. I deposited the money last night. If you would just take this check and hold it for ten days . . ."

"Certainly."

"That would leave me enough for taxes and to get the car washed, don't you think?"

"I should think so."

"Now, what was the amount again?"

"Three thousand, four hundred twenty-nine dollars and forty-seven cents."

"I thought we were forgetting about the forty-seven cents. The Relish Burger."

"Yes. All right."

"Every penny counts, you know."

Fletch wrote the check for three thousand, four hundred twenty-nine dollars payable to Linda Fletcher and signed it I.M. Fletcher in an illegible handwriting.

"There you are, Mr. Gillett. Thanks for stopping by. I'm sorry we're not on the seventh floor."

"It's been nice doing business with you, Mr. Fletcher."

Standing at the door, Gillett still held the check between his thumb and index finger. Fletch noticed that his clothes were weirdly cut—the man had no pockets. No pockets at all. How did he get around without pockets?

16

"By the way, Mr. Fletcher, I read your piece in the magazine regarding what you termed the unfairness of divorce settlements, alimony in particular."

"Thank you."

"I feel obliged to tell you what a stupid and wrong piece that was."

"Wrong?"

"Dead wrong."

"I understand your thinking so. You're a divorce lawyer. Why don't you take an advance in career and become a pimp?"

"I suspect that any divorce attorney, such as myself, could sue you for that piece and win."

"I quoted divorce attorneys."

"None I know."

"I'm only allowed to quote legitimate sources."

Before leaving, Gillett tried to look haughty, but only succeeded in looking as if he were in the early stages of a sneeze.

"Collins Aviation. Good morning."

"Good morning. I wish to talk with Mr. Stanwyk's secretary, please."

"One moment, please."

Beneath his desk, Fletch pried off his sneakers. The linoleum was cool on his bare feet.

"Mr. Stanwyk's office."

"Good morning. This is Bob Ohlson of the *Chronicle-Gazette*," Fletch said. "We're doing a little women's page feature over here, and wonder if you could help us out."

"Yes, certainly."

"This is just a silly little story, of no importance."

"I understand."

"What we're doing is a piece on who the private doctors are of prominent people around town. We thought it would amuse people."

"I see."

"I wonder if you could tell us who Mr. Stanwyk's private physician is?"

"Oh, I don't think Mr. Stanwyk would like to give out that information."

"Is he there?"

"Yes. He came in just a little while ago."

"You might tell him what we want. If we print the name of his doctor, Mr. Stanwyk probably will never get another doctor's bill. Remind Mr. Stanwyk that doctors themselves can't advertise."

"Yes, I see." The secretary's laugh indicated a finishing school with office skills. She had a finished laugh. "Hang on a moment, I'll see."

While he was waiting, Fletch took the envelope with ten one-hundred-dollar bills off his desk and threw it into a drawer.

"Mr. Ohlson? Mr. Stanwyk laughed and said it was all right to tell you that his private physician is Dr. Joseph Devlin of the Medical Center."

"That's great."

The man arranges for his own murder on Thursday night, and on Friday morning laughs at someone's wanting to know who his private physician is. At least Stanwyk had good blood pressure.

"When will the piece appear in the newspaper, Mr. Ohlson?"

"Well, we'll have to get a photograph of Dr. Devlin . . . "

"Can't you guess when? We'd love to see it."

"Friday of next week," Fletch said. "I think."

"Oh, that's fine. I'll tell Mr. Stanwyk so he'll be sure to buy the *Chronicle-Gazette* that day."

"Right. Be sure to buy the *Chronicle-Gazette*. Friday of next week."

Fletch hung up the phone of the *News-Tribune*.

Medical Center, Medical Center . . . Alan Stanwyk expects to be murdered next Thursday night. Failing that, he expects to pick up the *Chronicle-Gazette* Friday morning to read a reference to his private physician. Ah, life: neither was true . . . 553-9696.

"Medical Center. Good morning."

"Dr. Joseph Devlin's office, please."

"One moment."

"Dr. Devlin's office. Good morning."

"Good morning. Dr. Devlin, please."

"Dr. Devlin is seeing a patient. May I be of any assistance?"

18

"I need to speak with Dr. Devlin himself, I'm afraid."

"Oh, dear."

"We are the carriers of the life and health policies of Mr. Alan Stanwyk . . . "

"Oh yes."

"A little problem has come up regarding these insurance policies . . . "

"One moment, sir. I'll see if Dr. Devlin is free."

Fletch could hear the nurse-receptionist-secretary-whatever saying, "It's Mr. Stanwyk's insurance company. They have some question . . . "

Another phone was picked up instantly. "Yes?"

"Good morning, Dr. Devlin. As you know, we are the holders of policies on the life of Mr. Alan Stanwyk . . . "

"Yes."

"Who is a patient of yours?"

"In a manner of speaking."

"What does that mean?"

"Well, I'm the Collins' family doctor. John Collins and I were roommates in college. Stanwyk married his daughter, Joan Collins. So I guess I'm his physician. I usually only see him socially."

"How long has Mr. Stanwyk been your patient, doctor?"

"Since he moved out here. Really, since before he married Joan. I'm not being very specific, am I? About six years. I could look it up, if you like."

"No, that's all right, doctor. We're just reviewing some of these cases here. As you know, Mr. Stanwyk is insured for an enormous amount of money."

"Yes, I do know."

"Why is that, by the way? Why is he insured for so much?"

"Oh, that's John's doing. The kid, Alan, loves to fly these experimental planes. You know, he was in the Air Force before he went to business school. He kept up his flying and jumps at the chance to fly any ridiculous-looking thing somebody thinks will go up in the air. I guess his continuing to do so means something to the company. Collins Aviation."

"Would there be a three-million-dollar loss to the family if Mr. Stanwyk were killed?"

"I don't know. I suppose so. The stock would drop, and the family owns most of it. He's the fair-haired boy of the company, and there isn't any other. They would have management difficulties, personnel difficulties. . . . Yes, I suppose the family could lose that much if Alan were killed."

"I see."

"But, frankly, I don't think that's the reason for the policy."

"Oh?"

"John put that policy on him to try to get him to stop flying these gimcracked planes after Julia was born. He thought the premiums would convince Alan he should give up flying. I believe John mentioned that to me over a drink one day at the Racquets Club. I had said that much insurance on somebody would make anybody a target for murder. John didn't think my impugning his daughter was funny."

"Who is Julia?"

"The granddaughter. I mean, Joan's daughter. Joan and Alan. A cute little tyke."

"Mr. Stanwyk is still flying?"

"Oh, yes. Every once in a while we hear of a near scrape. Keep the insurance on."

"When was the last time you examined Mr. Stanwyk, doctor?"

"Not since before you guys took him over. You're giving him a complete physical every six months. How many times a year can a man be examined?"

"You haven't seen him at all?"

"As I say, just socially. At John's for drinks, or dinner at the club."

"What sort of shape would you say he is in?"

"I couldn't say without examining. From seeing him at the pool and in the locker room, I can say he is a slim, well-built young man, muscular and apparently perfectly healthy. He drinks and smokes moderately. He's built like a twenty-year-old boxer. Except for his wind, he could go fifteen rounds with anybody."

"Is it possible he could be seeing any doctor other than you?"

"Anything's possible."

"A specialist?"

"I don't know who would refer him to a specialist, if your insurance doctor didn't. And if he became aware of a problem, he would most likely refer him back to me, and I would refer him to a specialist, if he needed one. If the question is, have I referred him to a specialist lately, or ever, the answer is no."

"Thank you, doctor. Sorry to take your time."

"May I ask the reason for this inquiry?"

"We have to do a summary investigation of these large carriers periodically."

"Three million dollars is a hefty amount of insurance. That much insurance on a man would change his whole way of life, I would think."

"Or his way of death, doctor."

4

"Library."

"I asked for the clips on Alan Stanwyk at a quarter past eight this morning. It is now a quarter to eleven. What the hell's the matter with you people?"

"Is this Mr. Fletcher?"

"It is."

"The chief librarian wants to speak with you."

Fletch had been pleased to get the photo file on Stanwyk before the chief librarian had arrived for work at nine.

"Fletcher?"

"Yes."

"We have the clips on Alan Stanwyk down here for you anytime you want to pick them up."

"Terrific. Such cooperation. I've been waiting two hours while you guys have been playing games."

"Running a morgue is no game, Fletcher. We are not running a delivery service. You have to come down and get the file yourself."

"I said thank you."

"And you have to sign out the file yourself. I've had enough of your denials that you never took something that simply disappeared after it was delivered to you."

"I'll be right down. Try not to have the out-to-lunch sign up when I get there."

Fletch was halfway down the corridor to the library before he realized he had forgotten to put his sneakers back on.

"I would have brought the file to you myself, Mr. Fletcher, but Mr. Osborne said not to." The great round frames to her eyeglasses made the girl look almost attractive.

"Fuck Mr. Osborne."

"He has the file."

Osborne had a large red nose and always looked hung over. He had been a good reporter once.

"Here's where you sign, Fletch; thank you very much. And here's your file. Shitty piece you did last week on the bookie joints."

"Sorry."

"My joint was closed all week. Couldn't make a bet anywhere in town."

"Good for what's left of your character."

"I kept track of the races. I figure you lost me about five hundred dollars."

"I'll send you a check, I get paid so much."

"I'm just saying: thanks very much. Anytime I can do you a favor . . ."

"You can. Fuck off."

"Return this file before you go home, sweetheart, or I'll report you."

"I.M. Fletcher. Reporter."

"For now."

The girl with the nice glasses looked at his bare feet and smiled. "Fletcher!"

Clara Snow was in the corridor.

22

"For Christ's sake, Fletcher!"

Beige suit, alligator accessories, all trim and proper for a trim and proper day.

"You just getting in, Clara?"

"For Christ's sake, Fletcher, jeans and a T-shirt are bad enough; can't you wear shoes in the office?"

"I've been here since seven-thirty."

"You're not supposed to be here at all. You're supposed to be at The Beach."

"I told you last night I was coming up."

"And I told you not to come."

"I had to do some research."

"I don't give a damn. I told you not to leave The Beach until you had that story. Do you have the story?"

"No."

"Fletcher." In the dark of the corridor her face was clearly purple. "I'll talk to you later. I'm late for firing someone. Someone else."

"What? Did you and Frank oversleep?"

"That's not funny. It's not even amusing."

"That's your problem."

Fletch spread the file over his desk. The clips on Alan Stanwyk were from various sections of the newspaper, mainly society and financial, but also sports and run-of-paper. On each clip, Stanwyk's name was circled in red the first time it appeared.

Fletch snapped on the tape recorder he had brought from the passenger seat of his MG. His bare feet on the desk, he leaned back in his swivel chair.

"Eleven A.M. Friday. Re: The Murder Mystery.

"So far we have established only a few things.

"First, from the picture files at the *News-Tribune*, I have established that the man I met last night, who brought me to the Stanwyk house, was Alan Stanwyk.

"Second, he is executive vice president of Collins Aviation, married to Joan Collins and has one child, Julia, age hopefully somewhat less than six.

"His private physician and family friend, Dr. Joseph Devlin, of the Medical Center, confirms that Stanwyk is insured for three million dollars. The reason Devlin offers for the heavy insurance is that Stanwyk's father-in-law and company president, chairman of the board, wishes to discourage Stanwyk from continuing to fly experimental planes. So far, the discouragement induced by heavy premiums hasn't worked. Stanwyk is still flying.

"So far, we have not had a reliable check on Stanwyk's health. Nor do I think we're going to get one.

"Devlin pleaded ignorance regarding Stanwyk's physical condition, which is a queer thing for a family physician to do, unless he were covering himself.

"And, most significantly, the doctor indicated that Collins Aviation stock would fall if word got around that Alan Stanwyk is terminally ill. It's a safe bet the dear old family doctor and friend has a large slice of his savings in Collins Aviation.

"It would be to his benefit to lie and to give Stanwyk all the time possible to put his house in order.

"Therefore, it is unconfirmed and probably unconfirmable whether or not Alan Stanwyk has terminal cancer.

"To me he looked a healthy man, but I'm not better at medical diagnosis than I am at safecracking, to everyone's disappointment."

Leaning over the clips spread out on his desk, Fletch worked the on-off button on the tape recorder microphone.

"Let's see. From the *News-Tribune* clips, the Alan Stanwyk file, we have the following:

"Engagement is announced, Joan Collins to Alan Stanwyk, November, six years ago at a big bash at the Racquets Club.

"She is the daughter of John and Marion Collins. The only child. Graduated from The Hills High School, Godard Junior College, and took a year at the Sorbonne. Won Tennis Juniors when she was fifteen and sixteen. Since her year in France, worked in the International Department of Collins Aviation.

"The lady sounds dull.

"Alan Stanwyk, son of Marvin and Helen Stanwyk, Nonheagan, Pennsylvania. Colgate College, Bachelor of Arts degree. Captain,

United States Air Force, flew twenty-four missions in Indochina. Purple Heart. Graduated from Wharton Business School.

"At the time of the engagement he was assistant vice president of sales for Collins Aviation.

"January first, it is announced on the financial page that Alan Stanwyk is named executive vice president of Collins Aviation. The old man wanted to see how the boy worked out as a big man in the office before finding out how he worked out as a son-in-law.

"In April, Alan Stanwyk announced a multimillion-dollar government contract for Collins Aviation.

"Big wedding in June at the Collins family home in The Hills. Biographies are the same, but there is no reference to Stanwyk's family attending the wedding. Best man is Burt Eberhart, Colgate graduate, same year as Stanwyk.

"The Stanwyks, the Stanwyks . . . it is announced . . . Joan Stanwyk, Junior League, Symphony Friend . . . A dinner-dance benefit the Symphony at the Racquets Club, in fact, once a year: each October. Julia Collins Stanwyk born in March the year after the wedding. All very proper.

"But interesting: she's here, she's there, she's everywhere at first after becoming Mrs. Alan Stanwyk—teas, lunches, dinners, openings, cocktails. Yet either her activity declined steadily, or the society writers didn't find her very good copy. Which would be unusual, as she is née Collins and the average American blonde who takes a good picture.

"Apparently she has done very little the last six months.

"Oh, Mrs. Stanwyk . . . why have you withdrawn . . . at thirty?

"Alan Stanwyk. Sails as navigator on his father-in-law's yacht, the *Colette*, in the Triangle Race every year. Never won. Never placed. Skippered by John Collins. A sailing as well as a tennis-playing family. A very rich family.

"Alan Stanwyk becomes member of Racquets Club executive committee. Three years. Treasurer, Racquets Club, the last three years. Makes it to finals tournaments in both tennis and squash. Never wins. Never places.

"Becomes a member of the Urban Club. Reads a paper urging city police to return to foot patrols. Key phrase is: 'Get the cops out of their cars and back into the community.' Yeah, Stanwyk. The police chief answers. The mayor answers. People listen to Alan Stanwyk.

"The next year the paper he delivers to the Urban Club is in defense of jet noise around Collins Aviation. In answer to an earlier paper read to the Urban Club by my boss: *News-Tribune* editor-in-chief Frank Jaffe. Wonder who wrote it for him. Probably Clara Snow, over a cup of Ovaltine. No one answered Stanwyk that time.

"Stanwyk Speaks on F-111. He's in favor of them. Stanwyk Flies F-111 Simulator. Stanwyk Flies this and Stanwyk Flies that. Stanwyk tests Collins cold-weather private-plane equipment in Alaska.

"Stanwyk honored by U.S. aviation writers.

"Stanwyk, Stanwyk, Stanwyk . . . more of the same. I see why his father-in-law married him. There are no flies on Stanwyk. If there were, short of murder, somehow I doubt our sterling journal would print them . . ."

The telephone rang.

Fletch said into it, "So glad you called."

"Fletch, can't you do anything right? Like grow up?"

"Clara, darling! You sound relaxed and subdued, like just after sex. You just fired someone."

"As a matter of fact, I just did."

"Who?"

"A kid in the city room. He had been calling people up and asking them stupid questions, saying he was someone from the Associated Press."

"Really? How awful! I always tell people I'm from the *Chronicle-Gazette,* myself."

"I wouldn't be surprised."

"How did you catch the jerk?"

"He called the French embassy in Washington and asked how to spell *élan.* We got the bill."

"What awful snoops you are."

"He admitted it."

"And you fired him after he admitted it?"

"We can't have people doing that. AP complained."

"Jesus. I'll never confess to anything again."

"Fletcher, we have to talk."

"Are you up to it?"

"That's why I thought we should have lunch. In the cafeteria. Put your shoes on."

"You're not taking me out?"

"I wouldn't be seen in public with you. Even a drugstore lunch counter wouldn't let us in, the way you dress."

"If I had Frank's income . . ."

"Upstairs in the cafeteria, at least people will understand I'm eating with you because I have to."

"You don't have to. I have work to do."

"I have several things to talk to you about, Fletcher. Might as well get it over with. Including your Bronze Star."

"My Bronze Star?"

"See you upstairs. Put your shoes on."

5

Clara Snow had ordered an uncut bacon-lettuce-tomato sandwich on toast. When she bit into it the two edges of toast nearer Fletch gaped as if about to bite him.

"Tell me what I've always wanted to know, Clara, and somehow never expected to find out: how is our editor-in-chief, Frank Jaffe, in bed?"

"Fletch, why don't you like me?"

"Because you don't know what you're doing. You don't know anything about this business."

"I've been employed in this business a lot longer than you have."

"As a cooking writer. You know nothing about hard news. You know nothing about features. You know nothing about the mechanics of this business."

Speaking like a schoolmarm trying to coax a boy full of puberty toward the periodic tables, she said, "Are you sure you don't resent me just because I'm a woman?"

"I don't resent women. I rather like women."

"You haven't had much luck with them."

"My only mistake is that I keep marrying them."

"And they keep divorcing you."

"I don't even mind your going to bed with the editor-in-chief. What I do mind is your being made an editor—my editor—solely because you are going to bed with the editor-in-chief, when you are totally unqualified and, I might add, totally incompetent. Go to bed with Frank if you like. Anything to keep the bastard reasonably sober and relaxed. But your accepting an editorship in bed when you are unqualified is thoroughly dishonest of you."

Even in the cafeteria light, the skin over Clara's cheekbones as she stared at him was purple.

She bit into the sandwich, and the toast yawned at Fletch.

He chewed his calves' liver open-mouthed.

"Such principle," she said, sucking Coke from a straw. "You can't tell me you haven't made every strung-out little girl on the beach."

"That's different. That's for a story. I will do anything for a story. That's why I put penicillin on my expense account."

"You do?"

"Under 'Telephones.' "

"What Frank and I do together, and what our personal relationship is, is none of your damned business, Fletcher."

"Fine. I'll buy that. Just leave me alone, and leave my goddamned copy alone. You chopped hell out of my divorce equity story and made me look like a raving idiot."

"I had to make changes in it, and you were away on a story. I couldn't get in touch with you."

"It came out totally imbalanced, thanks to you, bitch editor. If I were a divorce lawyer in our circulation area, I would have sued the hell out of me by now. You opened me and the newspaper wide for suit, besides making me look like an incompetent."

"I tried to get in touch with you."

"Leave my copy alone. You don't know what you're doing."

"Want coffee?"

"I never take stimulants."

"For now, Fletch, we have to work together."

"Until you build enough of a case against me to get me fired, right?"

"Maybe. Now please tell me how you are doing on the drugs-on-the-beach story."

"There are drugs on the beach."

"Lots?"

"On that particular stretch of beach, lots."

"Hard drugs?"

"Very."

"Who are the people there?"

"The so-called kids on the beach are divided into two groups. The first group are drifters, kids on the road, alienated, homeless wanderers, usually incapable of permanent relationships. Some of them are just sun-worshippers, but if they are, they case this particular stretch of beach and move on. The kids who stay are there for the drugs. Because there is a source there, somewhere, of good, clean junk. Some of these so-called kids are forty years old. Although others aren't, like Bobbi."

"Tell me about Bobbi."

"Jesus, she's been listening. Bobbi is as cute as a button, only sexier. She is fifteen, blond, with a beautiful, compact little body."

"Have you been making it with her?"

"She needed someplace to crash."

"A fifteen-year-old. And you talk about me."

"She came out with a guy older than I am. Originally from Illinois. Daddy's a dentist. She fell in love with this guy passing through the local coffee shop, packed a knapsack and came with him. Once she was on the beach and thoroughly hooked, he wandered off. She was hooking when I met her."

"How are you paying for her?"

"Expense account. Under 'Breakfast' and 'Lunch.' "

"Aren't you afraid of the law, Fletcher? A fifteen-year-old?"

"If there is no one to complain for a kid, the law don't give a shit."

"Fletcher's Rule."

"The second group of kids on the beach are the local teenagers. They show up after school in their stripped Volkswagens, with surfboards, and make deals with daddy's hard-earned bread. The fuzz care a lot more about the local kids, as might be expected. In fact, one kid in particular, a kid named Montgomery, they pick up every week, yank him down for questioning. His dad is important in the town or something. Regular as clockwork. But he shows up again, almost immediately, beat up and smiling."

"Why do the kids go to that beach?"

"Because there is a source there."

"Who is the source?"

"An older drifter called Vatsyayana. I'd say he's in his mid-thirties. Balding and bearded. Oddly enough, he's got kindly eyes. Desperately skinny. The local kids call him Fat Sam."

"So why haven't you a story, if you know this much?"

"Because I don't know what Fat Sam's source is. I can't figure it out. He never seems to leave the beach. I spent ten days tailing him. All he seems to do is sell, sell, sell. I know where his stash is. It's in a chink of the sea wall. When word passed that Fat Sam was getting low, I kept my eyes on the stash for thirty-six hours. One: Fat Sam didn't leave the beach. Two: no one else went near his stash. After thirty-six hours, the supply was up again. Rationing was over. I can't figure it out."

"You missed the contact."

"Thanks."

"You've been on the story three weeks."

"That's not so much."

"Why don't we just run with what we've got? Put Fat Sam out of business?"

"Who cares about Fat Sam? The thing would start up again within a month. If you were any kind of a journalist, Clara, you would know we do not have a story until we have Fat Sam's source."

"You've got to stop somewhere. I mean, his source must have a source. Do you plan to follow the sources back to Thailand or some such place?"

"Maybe."

"You've got pictures of Fat Sam dealing, right?"

"Right."

"Let's run with it."

"Negative. You'll get the story when there is one. Putting one little pusher behind bars for twelve hours is not my idea of journalism."

"Frank is anxious."

"You're in charge of relieving Frank's anxieties."

"I wish I could have dessert," she said.

Fletch was eating a strawberry shortcake with whipped cream.

Clara said quickly, "There's a matter of insubordination. Disobedience."

Fletch put a perfect balance of strawberry shortcake and whipped cream on his fork.

"I told you not to leave The Beach today. One: we want you to stay there until that story is done. Two: we don't want you to blow your cover. Whoever Fat Sam's source is could be wise to you by this time, or suspicious. He could be watching you. All you needed to do was jump into your Alfa Romeo or whatever it is you drive, and speed up to the *News-Tribune*, which you have done, and you are dead."

"Good shortcake. It's an MG."

"What?"

"MG."

"I don't understand you."

"My car. It's an MG."

"Oh. You may be dead."

"I'll get the story in first."

"Do you think you should go back to The Beach?"

"Sure."

"Will you be safe?"

"Come with me and find out."

"No, thanks. But I do wonder, Fletch, if we hadn't ought to tell the local police that you're down there. Who you are and what you're doing."

Fletch put down his fork and sat back in his chair. His look was meant to terrify.

"If you do that, Clara, you'll be dead before me. I will kill you. Make no mistake."

"We're responsible for you, Fletcher."

"Then be responsible, goddamn it, and shut the fuck up! You never blow a story! To anyone, at any time, ever! Christ, I wish I didn't have to talk to you, you're such an idiot."

"All right, Fletcher, calm down. People are watching."

"I don't give a shit."

"I won't talk to the police—yet."

"Don't talk to the police or anyone else—ever. If I need help, I'll ask for it."

"All right, Fletcher. All right, all right, all right."

"Stupid bitch."

"Which brings up the last matter—your Bronze Star."

"What about it?"

"While you've been gone, not only have thousands of sleazy lawyers hired by your dozens of ex-wives been prowling the corridors ready to leap at you, but the marine commandant's office has been calling as well."

"So what."

"You won a Bronze Star."

"Years ago."

"You never picked it up."

"Right."

"May I ask why not?"

"Such a thing doesn't belong in a pawnshop."

"What do you mean?"

"That's where they all end up, isn't it?"

"I don't see why."

"You don't have so many ex-wives."

"You are going to pick up the Bronze Star."

"I am not."

"It's all arranged. There is to be a ceremony next Friday, a week from today, in the commandant's office at the marine base, and you are going to be there in a suit and tie *and* shoes."

"What the hell is this to you? This is private business."

"It is not private business. You are I.M. Fletcher, star writer of the *News-Tribune,* and we are going to have a photographer there and a cub reporter and we are going to run you smiling modestly in all editions Saturday."

"You are like hell."

"We are. What's more, the marine commandant is going to have his full public relations staff, including photographers, there."

"No."

"And we're going to try to make a wire story out of it and tell the whole world both about your exploits and the modesty that has kept you from picking up such a high honor all these years. We won't tell them you really haven't picked it up just because basically you are a slob."

"I won't be done with The Beach story by then."

"You will turn in your beach story, whatever it looks like, with pictures, by four o'clock Thursday afternoon. We will run it in the Sunday paper, with a little sidebar saying, *News-Tribune* reporter I.M. Fletcher received the Bronze Star Friday, etc."

"You will do nothing of the sort."

"Frank has decided. The publisher has agreed."

"I don't care. I haven't."

"There is the matter of insubordination. You left an assignment when you were told clearly not to."

"I won't do it."

"I'll put it more simply, Fletcher: you have The Beach story in, complete, Thursday afternoon at four and be in the marine commandant's office next Friday morning at ten, or you're fired. And I, for one, will cheer."

"I bet you will."

"You're an obnoxious prick."

"I sell newspapers."

"You heard me, Fletcher. Thanks for wearing your shoes to lunch."

"I didn't."

6

"Fletcher, this is Jack Carradine. I tried to call you earlier, but apparently you were out to lunch."

"I just ran upstairs to get bitten."

"What?"

"I was in the cafeteria getting chewed out."

"I have some information for you regarding Alan Stanwyk, but before I give it to you I'd like to know what you want it for. The financial department of this newspaper can't be totally irresponsible."

"Of course. I understand." Fletch switched the telephone to his left ear and picked up a pen. "The truth is," he lied, "we're thinking we might do a feature story on who the most highly, I should say heavily, insured people are in this area and why they are so heavily insured."

"Is Alan Stanwyk heavily insured?"

"Yes. Very heavily."

"It stands to reason. He has a lot riding on his nose. Who is the beneficiary?"

"Wife and daughter, I believe."

"I shouldn't think they'd need the money. But since they hold a lot of stock in Collins Aviation, which he runs almost single-handedly, I suppose they would suffer at least a temporary loss upon his passing."

"Right," Fletcher drawled. "What have you got?"

"Well, as I just told you, he runs Collins Aviation. He's the executive vice president—has been since he married his wife. His father-in-law is president and chairman of the board, but he really leaves the running of the company to Stanwyk. It is expected that within two or three years, once he gets a little age on him, he will be made president of Collins. His father-in-law is only in his late fifties but would rather sail his yacht and run tennis tournaments. He seems to trust Stanwyk completely."

"How is the company doing?"

"Beautifully. The stock, what there is of it available, is high and solid. Never been higher, in fact. They declared a stock dividend last year. They're considered a little weak in management, but that doesn't matter so much when you have a man as young and as competent as Stanwyk running the show. And he does, absolutely. He's a hard-working fellow. It is presumed that as his father-in-law's executive team begins to retire in the next few years, Stanwyk will bring in his own fresh young team. It won't be hard for him to do so, because he has made a point of knowing almost everybody in the industry."

"Mind a stupid question?"

"I'm used to them."

"What does Collins Aviation do?"

"They design and manufacture subsidiary parts for airplanes. In other words, they don't make airplanes, but they might make the seats, or engine parts, or control panels, what have you. Without meaning to make a pun, they also have a satellite division that does the same thing for spacecraft. This latter division has grown terrifically under Stanwyk. Apparently he is an attractive, amiable, personable man who always seems to be able to get the right contract for his company at the right time. Someone said, 'He's firm, but he never presses.' "

"How much is a company like that worth?"

"To whom?"

"I mean, what is its net worth?"

"Well, Fletch, you don't really know what you mean. Companies aren't houses that have an approximate aggregate value. Companies are worth precisely what their stock is worth on the market at that moment. It has a considerable gross income, a nifty net return to the stockholders, a big payroll . . ."

"Gimme a figure."

"If it were a house? If it were a house, Collins Aviation might be worth a half a billion."

"Half a billion dollars?"

"Can you count that high?"

"Not even with my shoes off. Who owns it?"

"The Collins family—John, his wife and daughter—continue to own fifty-one per cent of the company."

"Wow."

"They are very rich. Of course, the stock is actually held in foundations and trusts and what-have-you, but it's all John Collins when it comes time to vote. I must add that the Collins family, so you won't think they're complete dopes, have an amount equal to or greater than their investment in Collins Aviation invested through investment houses in Boston."

"Phew. Why Boston?"

"You don't know much, do you, Fletcher?"

"Not about money. I've seen so little of it."

"Boston is the Switzerland of this hemisphere. It is chock-a-block full of quiet, conservative investment bankers."

"I thought it was full of beans."

"It is. Other people's."

"How do people get as rich as Collins?"

"If I knew, do you think I'd be sitting here? Collins is a Harvard graduate who started designing and making airplane equipment with his own hands in a rented garage on Fairbanks Avenue in the early 1930s. Patents led to capital. It's easy. Go do it. Everybody says he's a nice man, quiet, humble. He's good to his friends. Most of the rest of Collins Aviation stock is held by friends of the family. They're all as rich as lords. He's made heavy contributions to Harvard College, the Cancer Fund, muscular dystrophy . . ."

"The Cancer Fund?"

"He's given them something like a total of ten million dollars."

"Recently?"

"Yes. Continuously."

"I see."

"Stanwyk is the perfect man to be Collins's son-in-law, considering Collins doesn't have a son of his own. Stanwyk is from a modest family in Pennsylvania. His father is in the hardware business."

"Still alive?"

"I believe so. Why do you ask?"

"His parents didn't come out to his wedding."

36

"Probably couldn't afford it. That would have been an expensive trip for them."

"Stanwyk could have paid."

"There could have been lots of reasons why his parents didn't come to his wedding—ill health, business, cost—how do I know?"

"Go on."

"A brilliant student all the way through, and apparently a nice kid. True blue. A Boy Scout; a Golden Gloves champion for the state of Pennsylvania who did not go on to the nationals for some reason; summa cum laude at Colgate, where he did not box but began to play racquet sports; an Air Force flier who flew lots of missions, currently a major in the Air Force Reserves; graduated third in his class from Wharton Business School, which, because you probably don't know, is one of the best; came out here; worked in the sales department of Collins Aviation, where sales immediately jumped; became a vice president at twenty-six or twenty-seven; and married the boss's daughter. Apparently just a magnificent young man in all ways."

"He sounds machine-made."

"Too good to be true, huh? There are people like that. Unquestionably the guy is ambitious, but there is nothing immoral in that. He's done well and he's well liked."

"By the way, Jack, who is your source for all this?"

"I thought you'd never ask. The Collins family has a local stockbroker, an investment man out here who does just little things for them, you know, regarding Collins Aviation stock—little things that run into the millions—name of Bill Carmichael. We play golf together. Needless to say, Carmichael is the son of an old buddy of John Collins. His father died, and Carmichael fell heir to the account. He and Stanwyk have become close friends. Stanwyk has taken him flying. They play squash and tennis together. He genuinely likes Stanwyk. And, incidentally, he says Stanwyk genuinely likes his wife, Joan Collins, which ain't always the case."

"There is no hanky-panky going on?"

"Not as far as Carmichael knows. Between you and me, Stanwyk would have to be out of his mind to be playing around on the side under these circumstances. God knows what Papa would say if Stanwyk got thrown out of bed."

"Does Stanwyk have any money of his own?"

"No, not to speak of. He has savings from his salary invested with Carmichael, but it doesn't amount to much over a hundred thousand dollars."

"Poor fellow."

"He did not buy the house on Berman Street. She did, but it's in both their names. Carmichael says it's worth maybe a million dollars. However, Stanwyk maintains the house and staff, and supposedly all other family expenses, out of salary. Male chauvinist pride, I guess. Which is why he probably doesn't have more savings out of salary. That's an expensive family to keep up with. Incidentally, the house on Berman Street backs onto the Collins estate on, would you believe it, Collins Avenue?"

"Old John Collins has spyglasses."

"I gather there is a lot of back and forth."

"Doesn't he own a second house anywhere?"

"No. His father-in-law has a house in Palm Springs, one in Aspen, and one in Antibes. The kids use these houses whenever they like."

"Does he own his own airplane?"

"No. Collins Aviation has three Lear jets, with pilots, but Stanwyk flies them when he likes. He also has to do some flying to keep up his Air Force Reserve rank. And he flies experimental planes all over the country, supposedly to test Collins equipment. Carmichael suspects he just gets a kick out of it.

"Stanwyk is also the holder of some stock options in Collins Aviation. So I guess if you put everything together, he is probably a millionaire in his own right at this point, but it's on paper. He couldn't raise a million in cash without upsetting an awful lot of people.

"Oh, I forgot to tell you, Fletcher. Stanwyk and his wife have just converted about three million dollars of her personal stock."

"Converted?"

"Into cash. Carmichael says they intend to buy a cattle ranch in Nevada. He thinks it's an effort to get out from under the heel of Daddy Collins—go do their own thing."

38

"Is this Stanwyk's idea?"

"Carmichael has the impression it's her idea. At least, she's the one who likes horses. One can have enough of tennis and yachting, you know."

"I didn't know. Why cash?"

"The ranch costs something like fifteen million dollars."

"I can't get used to these figures."

"Inflation, my boy."

"How can a farm be worth fifteen million dollars?"

"Farms can be worth a lot more than that."

"Has Carmichael said anything to you about Stanwyk's health?"

"No. Except that he's a hell of a squash player. You have to be in pretty good shape to play that game. I tried it once. Twelve minutes and I was wiped out. Golf for me. Is there anything wrong with Stanwyk's health?"

"Would it matter if there were?"

"It would matter a lot. I have already mentioned to you that there is a kind of middle-management crisis at Collins Aviation. The whole thing now rests on the shoulders of one Alan Stanwyk. Old John Collins could go back to work, I suppose, but he never was as good a businessman as Stanwyk. He was an inventor who had some luck. Collins now has to be run by a real pro—which Daddy John ain't."

"Would the stock market fall if word got around that Stanwyk was terminally ill?"

"Collins stock sure would. That sort of thing would be very upsetting to that company. Executive personnel would start jockeying for position. Some would leave outright. Things would have to be in a state of confusion for about as long as Stanwyk has been running the place."

"I see. So if he were ill, I mean terminally ill, it would have to be kept a deep, dark secret."

"Absolutely. Is he ill?"

"How would I know?"

"Oh, I forgot. You're working on the insurance angle. Well, young Fletcher, I've told you everything I know about Alan Stanwyk. You see, we are not very close yet to the moneyless state you write about. There is still plenty of it around."

"I guess so."

"Stanwyk seems to be a competent, decent man who happened to marry the boss's daughter. Okay? Mind if I go back and do my own work now?"

"I appreciate your help very much."

"I'm just trying to prevent your writing one of your usual shitty pieces. Anything I could do would be worth that."

7

Fletch sat on the desk of The Beauty in the Broad-Brimmed Hat, Mrs. Amelia Shurcliffe, Society Editor. He had never heard that there was a Mr. Shurcliffe. Working at her typewriter, her forearms quivered with Who was at the most recent party and Are they getting married.

She finally deigned to notice the one-hundred-sixty-pound object on her desk.

"Why, Fletch! Aren't you beautiful! You always look just right. Faded jeans and T-shirt. Even no shoes. The Shoe Institute wouldn't like my saying this, and of course I'd never write it, but that's exactly what Style should be. Well, darling. Is."

"You're kidding, of course."

"Darling, I'm not."

"You should tell Clara Snow."

"Clara Snow. What does she know? She used to write cooking, you know. And between us, darling, she was terrible at that. Did you ever try to put together one of her 'Recommended Meals'?"

"Somehow, no."

"Desperate, just desperate. The colors all clashed. We tried it once, just for fun, some friends and I at the cottage. We ended up with a Hollandaise sauce, and you know what kind of a yellow that is, and carrots and beets, purple beets, all on the same plate. It was so garish, darling, we had to look away. We ate with our eyes averted. The tastes of things didn't go together either. I believe her cooking column was successful only with blind polar bears."

"You know, she's my editor now."

"Yes, I do know, you poor darling. If she weren't going to bed with Frank we would have upchucked her years ago. Of course Frank has very poor taste, too. Pink shirts and strawberry suspenders. Have you ever seen his wife?"

"Yes."

"A dowdy old thing. She always reminds me of an Eskimo full of baked beans. I mean, she looks as if, if she ever got unfrozen, she would evaporate in one enormous fart."

"Have you ever told her so?"

"Oh, no, darling, I wouldn't. I can't go to bed with her husband, being both overage and overweight, but that doesn't mean I can insult his wife. Somehow it all doesn't matter to me. Frankly, darling, I find Frank as attractive as a hangover. You're much more my type: lean, healthy, stylish."

"I'm horrified at the thought that you think I'm stylish."

"But I do, darling, sincerely. Your style is exactly what Beau Brummel did in his time. All Brummel did, you know, was to bring the lean, simple country style into the city."

"No, I didn't know."

"You should talk with Amelia Shurcliffe more. You see how simple your clothes are; how clean the lines: jeans and T-shirt. Blue and white. The lines couldn't be cleaner. You're not wearing shoes in the newspaper office, which is about as downtown as one can get. Here you can feel the whole city throbbing around you. And you're dressed as if in the middle of a hayloft. Delightful style. Just right."

"I'm amazed."

"Who does your hair?"

"No one."

"What do you mean, 'no one'?"

"When it sticks out someplace, I chop it off."

"Delightful. You're darling."

Amelia Shurcliffe was dressed in a tailored blue suit and white blouse. It was obvious she was liberated enough not to wear a corset. Her belly bulged from too many lunches and cocktail parties a week. The henna of her hair matched her face.

41

"Well, Fletch, I'm sure you didn't come along simply to have me admire you. You could go anywhere for that. What can I do for you?"

"Alan Stanwyk."

"Joan and Alan Stanwyk. This area's most exciting couple. No, I shouldn't say that. They're beautiful, bright, healthy and rich. But come to think of it, they don't really do anything. In fact, thinking of how exciting they could be, the Stanwyks may be this area's dullest couple."

"Which are they? Exciting or dull?"

"Rather dull, I think. He married her for Collins Aviation, of course."

"You say that straight out?"

"Well, I suppose someone had to marry her, of course. And she's attractive enough, if you like the usual American leggy blonde."

"I do, actually."

"I'm sure you do. I was one, once. Not all that leggy, of course. I was more petite. But Joan Collins Stanwyk is sort of boring, I think. I mean, she's Symphony, of course; gives that bash once a year at the Racquets Club to raise money for the violinists' rosin supply or something, and he always shows up and they stand in the receiving line and all that. Californian Gothic, if you know what I mean. They never seem to be enjoying themselves. They show up at dinners and cocktails, that sort of thing. They never seem to speak unless spoken to. They always seem to be just going through the motions."

"They must do something for fun. I mean, for themselves."

"No, I honestly think they are too busy being ideal. Perhaps they're too aware of their position. I understand he sincerely likes flying. But all the rest of it, the racquet sports, the sailing, what-have-you, seems forced somehow for them. Of course all that money must be oppressive."

"It must be."

"Jack Collins, her father, is a nifty man. Attractive, bright. I've always been slightly in love with him. Of course he's my generation. But one has always had the idea from him, even when he's being formal, that somehow, maybe somewhere else in his mind, he's having fun. Of course his wife, Marion, is a bit tipsy. Never could hold

42

her liquor. Each year they keep her more restrained. That's why I've always thought Joan must mean so much to her father. You see them together at parties, Joan and her father—you know, benefits for cancer, or muscular dystrophy, or some of his other charities—and you always understand that Alan Stanwyk is off being busy with Collins Aviation. Sometimes he makes an appearance just at the end of an evening.

"Joan is in a difficult position, between her father and her husband." Amelia Shurcliffe took a hairpin from her desk drawer and applied it arbitrarily. "Perhaps that's why I think she's never having much fun."

"She has to be hostess for both of them."

"Yes. Instead of being herself, she has to have one hand working for Jack, the other for Alan."

"Reading through your clips, Amelia, on the Stanwyks, it appears Joan Stanwyk has been doing less and less in recent months, making fewer and fewer appearances."

"I suppose you're right."

"At least her name appears in your column less and less frequently."

"Now that you mention it, I'm sure you're right. She has been fading from the scene."

"Why?"

"It could mean many things. She has a child, a little daughter. She could be spending time with her. Joan could be pregnant. She could be worried about her husband. Seeing I have this idea that she doesn't enjoy herself, she could just be bored with the whole round. It has no novelty for her. She's been doing it since she came out, you know, with her father—unofficially acting as his hostess."

"You said she could be worried about her husband. What did you mean?"

"Oh, gracious. What did I mean? Well, her husband, Alan Stanwyk, is running an enormous company, and at an early age. That's an enormous responsibility, you know. He must work very hard and very long. And you know some of these fellows who always show a cool, pleasant face to the world are only able to do so because they fuss and fume at their wives in the privacy of their homes. If anything is wrong with him, she would know it."

"You mean if he were sick?"

"Physically sick?"

"Yes."

"I hardly think so. He looks the picture of health. Always."

"A possible explanation of her withdrawing from society in recent months is that she knows he is very sick."

"I suppose so. Is he?"

"How would I know?"

"Of course. You could speculate endlessly. Maybe she loves him and hates his risking his life in those airplanes all the time. His flying must be a worry to her."

"Amelia, do you think the Stanwyks love each other?"

"I always think so unless I know differently. Why shouldn't they?"

"Well, she seems to be half-married to her father, the wonderfully attractive Jack Collins. It looks to me as if Jack Collins picked Alan Stanwyk to be his daughter's husband. Alan Stanwyk married Collins Aviation instead of a girl named Joan Collins."

Amelia's eyes were the sort one told the truth to; simultaneously they appeared concerned and skeptical.

"Fletch, let me tell you something remarkable. In fact, the most remarkable thing I know. Are you ready for it?"

"All ears."

"I've been a society writer and professional busybody almost all my adult years, and the most remarkable thing I have learned is that people love each other when they have the least reason to, and when you least expect them to. Love-matches, marriages made in heaven, work no better than marriages made in board rooms. Obviously, the Stanwyks' marriage was made by Alan Stanwyk and Jack Collins. Joan just sort of got dragged along. Yet it is entirely possible that she is very much in love with Alan Stanwyk. Do you believe that?"

"If you say so."

"I'm not saying it's true, Fletch. I'm just saying it's possible. Joan and Alan might be terrifically in love with each other."

"Could Alan have a mistress?"

44

"Of course."

"Would John Collins understand?"

"Of course. I expect neither one of them feels confined to the marital bed. Not in this day and age."

"And you say John Collins would understand."

"Darling: the things I could tell you about John Collins. He didn't spend all his time in that garage twisting propellers."

"Sometimes men feel differently where their daughters are concerned. I had a father-in-law once."

"He wasn't Jack Collins."

"One more question, Amelia: why didn't Stanwyk's parents come for Alan's wedding?"

"My gracious, darling, you young folks do do your research, don't you? I have no idea. I suppose they felt they would have gotten eaten alive."

"Eaten alive?"

"Socially, darling. I suppose they're nobodies from Middle America and would have felt dreadfully out of place."

"Do people still feel that way?"

"Older people do, darling. You'll see."

"I wouldn't miss the wedding of my only child."

"Perhaps our young protagonist, Alan Stanwyk, kept them away for fear they would embarrass him. Maybe their grammar ain't no good. I don't have answers, Fletcher, to all of your questions. I remember at the wedding, whenever it was, six or seven years ago, there was a vague interest in meeting the Stanwyks, but it was explained, if you can call it an explanation, that the Stanwyks couldn't make it. End of vague interest. Maybe they had dentists' appointments that day."

"Amelia, you're a peach. Thank you very much."

"I do have a bone to pick with you, young Fletcher, despite my otherwise unrestrained approval of you."

"Oh oh."

"Has to do with that piece you wrote a couple of months ago, a little ditty called something fresh and original like 'Society is Dead.' "

"I'm not any more responsible for headlines than you are, Amelia."

"You are partly responsible, however, for the unadulterated rubbish that dribbles down from your by-line."

"Yes. Partly."

"That piece was rubbish, Fletcher."

"Oh?"

"Society, as you see, is not dead. There is plenty of it about. Just because you found a few grandnieces and nephews of prominent people hanging about the street corners sniffing pot, or whatever you do with it, saying too loudly and too frequently that they don't care anymore proves nothing. You haven't been reading me."

"Amelia, I've read every word of yours."

"Society changes, Fletcher, but not much. It does not die. It moves. It oozes. It changes its shape, its structure, its leaders and its entertainments. There is always a Society. As long as the instinct for power beats in the breasts of men and women, there will be a restricted clawing called Society."

"And there will always be a society columnist called Amelia Shurcliffe."

"Go off to bed with someone nice, darling, and be sure to tell her how I envy her."

8

"Trans World Airlines."

"Good afternoon. This is Irwin Fletcher. I asked my office to make a reservation for me today for your flight to Buenos Aires next Thursday night at eleven o'clock. My secretary has left for the weekend, and I just wanted to check and make sure it had been done."

"The name again, please, sir?"

"Fletcher. Irwin Fletcher."

"Flight 629 to Buenos Aires. Departure time eleven P.M. Thursday. Prepaid."

"Do you have a reservation on that flight for Irwin Fletcher?"

46

"Yes, sir. The reservation was made this morning. It will not be necessary to confirm the reservation again."

"Information. What city, please?"
"In Nonheagan, Pennsylvania, the number for Marvin Stanwyk, please."
"All our numbers are Pennsylvania numbers, sir."
"In Nonheagan."
"In which county is Nonheagan, sir?"
"I don't know. I'm not in Pennsylvania."
"How do you spell it, sir?"
"P-e-n-n-s-y-l—"
"I mean the name of the town, sir."
"Oh. N-o-n—"
"I found it, sir. It's in Bucks County."
"Thank you."
"When people call long-distance information, they are usually calling for Bucks County."
"That's damned interesting."
"Now, what is the name you wanted?"
"Stanwyk. Marvin Stanwyk. S-t-a-n-w-y-k."
"That's the wrong way to spell Stanwyk, sir."
"I'll tell him."
"We have a Stanwyk Marvin on Beecher Road."
"Do you have any other Stanwyk Marvin?"
"We have a Stanwyk Hardware on Ferncroft Road, also misspelled."
"Let me have both numbers, will you?"
"Yes, sir. They're both listed in Nonheagan."

"Mr. Stanwyk? This is Casewell Insurers of California, subinsurers of the subsidiary carriers of a partial policy listed by Alan Stanwyk, who is your son?"
"Yes."
"Glad to catch you in, sir."
"I'm always in."

47

"Just a few questions, sir. Are you and your wife currently alive?"

"Last time I looked, you damn fool."

"And you're both in good health?"

"Except for a pain in the ass from answering damn fools on the telephone."

"Thank you, sir. And you are the parents of Alan Stanwyk, executive vice president of Collins Aviation?"

"Unless my wife knows somethin' she never told me."

"I see, sir."

"I don't think they should let people like you dial long-distance."

"Very amusing, sir."

"I mean, you must be costing someone a passel of money."

"It's all paid for by the premiums, sir."

"That's what I was afraid of. Some other damn fool, like my son, is paying those premiums just so you can be a jackass coast-to-coast."

"Quite right, sir."

"It's damn fools like you who make me invest in telephone stock."

"Very wise of you, sir, I'm sure."

"The telephone company's the only outfit in the whole country making any money. It's because of fools like you some other fool lets near a telephone. Notice the way I'm keeping you talking?"

"I do, sir. You must own telephone stock."

"I do. Plenty of it. You didn't reverse the charges, did you?"

"No, sir. I didn't."

"Well, you'll be glad to know that both my wife and I are alive. Thanks to telephone stock and damn fools like you."

"When was the last time you saw your son, sir?"

"A few weeks ago."

"A few weeks ago?"

"He drops by every six weeks or so."

"Alan?"

"That's his name. My wife thought it was an improvement on Marvin, although I've never been sure."

"Your son, Alan, visits you in Pennsylvania every six weeks?"

"About that. Give or take a week. He has his own Collins Aviation planes. Jets. A nice young copilot comes with him who just loves

48

Helen's buckwheat cakes. He puts away three plates of them a morning and wants them again for lunch."

"Your son, Alan Stanwyk, flies across country every six weeks in a private jet to visit you?"

"He never was much of a letter-writer. Sometimes he's on his way in or out of New York or Washington."

"Not always?"

"No. Not always. Sometimes he just comes by."

"Then why weren't you at his wedding?"

"How do you know we weren't?"

"Insurance men know some funny things, Mr. Stanwyk."

"They must."

"Why weren't you at the wedding?"

"It's none of your business, even if you are an insurance man, but the answer is that the time got mixed up. We were supposed to go to Antigua for a vacation. Alan was paying. He was doing all right at Collins Aviation. A vice president of sales while he was twenty-something. That didn't surprise me any. I've always been strong in sales myself. So we said all right. We'd never had a real get-on-an-airplane vacation before. The wedding was supposed to be a week after we returned. Smack dab in the middle of our vacation, we get this telegram saying the wedding had been moved forward because of some big business shift in her Daddy's schedule. I think his name is John. We checked the airport, and no connection could be made until the next morning. The wedding was over. We missed it. I sorely would have loved to be there, though. The wife cried a little, but I figure she would have spilled a few tears even if she were there."

"You've never met the Collinses?"

"Never had the pleasure. I'm sure they're nice folks. I've never even met my daughter-in-law. Alan says she hates to fly. Isn't that the damnedest? Her Daddy owns an airplane company and her husband's a pilot and she won't get on an airplane."

"You've never been to California?"

"Nope. But we see a lot of it on television. Especially San Francisco. That place must be an awful pain in the ass to walk up and down. Hills and hills. Everybody in San Francisco must be either slope-shouldered or pigeon-breasted. Now, son, what did you call for?"

"That's all, sir."

"What's all?"

"Just inquiring about you and your wife."

"Seems to me we haven't had a conversation at all."

"If I think of anything more, I'll call back."

"Look here, son, if you think of anything at all, call back. I'd be relieved to hear you're thinking."

"I do have one other question, sir."

"I'm breathless waitin'."

"As far as you know, is your son in good health?"

"When he was fifteen years old, he fought the state Golden Gloves. He's been in better shape every year."

"You think he could win the Golden Gloves championship now?"

"That's not even funny, son."

"Mr. Stanwyk?"

"I'm still listening."

"I won the Bronze Star."

Fletch listened to the silence.

"I take back everything I said, son. Good for you."

"Thank you, sir."

"It's a pleasure being called by you. Is there any chance of your coming east with Alan?"

"He doesn't know me."

"He should. He won a Purple Heart. That doesn't mean as much. He just got in the way of something."

"So did I."

"I bet. I bet you did."

"Where was he wounded?"

"He crashed. A helicopter picked him up. The helicopter crashed. Busy snipers, that part of the woods. In the second crash a piece of metal went into his stomach. He told me it looked like an Amish door hinge. No one ever knew where it came from. Maybe the helicopter. I think it's possible it came from the first crash. A man can carry a door hinge for a while without knowing about it. It's okay. Recovering from it has kept him slim."

50

"Mr. Stanwyk?"

"Yes, son."

"If you were my dad, I'd pick up the Bronze Star next week."

"You never picked it up?"

"No, sir."

"You must have won it a while ago."

"I did. A long while ago."

"You ought to pick it up. Give the country a boost."

"I don't think so."

"What's your name, son, anyway?"

"James," Fletch said. "Sidney James."

9

RESERVED CAPTAIN PRECINCT THREE

Fletch parked there.

He went straight to the bull room.

"Lupo's in back," the sergeant at the typewriter said. "Beating the shit out of a customer."

"I'd hate to interrupt him. Someone might read the customer his rights."

"Oh, they've been read to him already. Lupo's interpretation of the Supreme Court ruling has been read to him."

"How does Lupo's interpretation go?"

"You've never heard it? It's really funny. I can't remember all of it. He rattles it off. Something like: 'You have the right to scream, to bleed, to go unconscious and call an attorney when we get done with you; visible injuries, including missing teeth, will be reported, when questioned, as having occurred before we picked you up, et cetera, et cetera.' It scares the shit out of people."

"I bet."

The sergeant picked up a phone.

"Lupo? Mr. I.M. Fletcher of the *News-Tribune* is here." The sergeant slid the heavy I.B.M. carriage to three-quarters across the page, punched one key, returned and tabbed once. "Okay."

He hung up and smiled happily at Fletch.

"Lupo said he made a bust Wednesday especially for you. Three dimes' worth for twenty dollars."

"Twenty dollars?"

"He says it's Acapulco Gold. You should be so lucky. It was a bust on advertising executives."

"I pity the poor bastards."

"You don't need three bags full to convict. It's in the second left-hand drawer of his desk."

Fletch took the plastic bag from the second left-hand drawer of the first desk in the third row from the windows.

"Thanks very much."

"The money, Lupo said."

"Do you accept credit cards?"

"Cash. It's for the Police Athletic Fund. Believe me, with his new chick, he needs an athletic fund."

"I believe you. Beating up people all day in the questioning room is a tough way to make a living."

"It's hard work."

"Sweaty."

Fletch dropped two tens on the sergeant's desk.

"We're going to try it on you, one day, I.M. Fletcher. Find out what the hell the initials I.M. stand for."

"Oh, no," Fletch said. "That's a secret that will go with me to my grave."

"We'll find out."

"Never. Only my mother knew, and I murdered her to keep her quiet."

Fletch sat in the sergeant's side chair.

"Seeing Lupo isn't here at the moment, and can't be disturbed," Fletch said slowly, "I wonder if you would give me a quick reading on a name."

"What name?" The sergeant put his hand on the phone.

"Stanwyk. W-Y-K. Alan. One '1.' "

"You looking for anything in particular?"

"Just a computer inquiry. A read-out."

"Okay." The sergeant dialed a short number on his phone and spelled the name slowly. He waited absently a moment and then listened, making notes on his pad. He hung up within three minutes.

"Stanwyk, Alan," he said, "has a six-month-old unpaid parking ticket in Los Angeles. Eleven years ago, Air Force Lieutenant Alan Stanwyk, while flying a training craft, buzzed a house in San Antonio, Texas. Complaint was transferred to Air Force, which reprimanded said Stanwyk, Alan."

"That's all?"

"That's all. I'm surprised, too. I seem to recognize the name from somewhere. He must be a criminal. The only names I ever see are the names of baddies."

"You might have seen it in the sports pages," Fletch said, getting up.

"Oh, yeah?"

"Yeah. He tried out for Oakland once."

Fletch went home.

His apartment was on the seventh floor of a building that had everything but design.

His apartment—a living room, a bedroom, bath and kitchenette—was impeccably neat. On the wall over the divan was a blow-up of a multiple *cartes-de-visite* by Andre Adolphe Eugene Disderi.

In the bathroom, he dropped his clothes in the laundry hamper and showered. The night before, after being away from his apartment for weeks, he had spent forty-five minutes in the shower.

Naked, he added the day's mail to the stack that had been waiting for him the night before on the coffee table. Sitting on the divan, he rolled himself a joint from the bag supplied by Police Detective Herbert Lupo.

A half hour later he picked up the stack of mail, unopened, and dropped it into the wastebasket beside the desk in his bedroom. They were all bills.

The phone rang.

Fletch shoulder-rolled onto the bed and answered it.

"Fletch?"

"My God. If it isn't my own dear, sweet wifey, Linda Haines Fletcher."

"How are you, Fletch?"

"Slightly stoned."

"That's good."

"I've already paid you today."

"I know. Mr. Gillett called and told me you had given him a great big check."

"Mr. Gillett? Of that distinguished law firm, Jackass, Asshole and Gillett?"

"Thank you, Fletch. I mean, for the money."

"Why do you call Gillett 'Mr.'? His pants don't even have pockets."

"I know. Isn't he awful?"

"I never thought you'd leave me for a homosexual divorce lawyer."

"We're just friends."

"I'm sure you are. So why are you calling me?"

Linda paused. "I miss you, Fletch."

"Jesus."

"It's been weeks since we've been together. Thirteen weeks."

"The cat must have decomposed by now."

"You shouldn't have thrown the cat through the window."

"Anyhow, I bought you lunch more recently than that. You think I'm made of money?"

"Together. I mean together."

"Oh."

"I love you, Fletch. You don't get over that in a minute."

"No. You don't."

"I mean, we had some beautiful times together. Real beautiful times."

"You know, around here now you can't even smell the cat."

"Remember the time we just headed off in your old Volvo and we lived in it a whole week? We didn't bring clothes, money, anything?"

"Credit cards. We brought credit cards."

"Do you still have the old Volvo?"

54

"No. An MG."

"Oh? What color is it?"

"It's called 'enviable green.' "

"I've been trying to get you on the phone."

"Even before you got your check?"

"Yes. Have you been away?"

"Yes. I've been working on a story."

"You've been gone a long time."

"It's a long story."

"What's it about?"

"Migrant workers' labor dispute."

"That doesn't sound very interesting."

"It isn't."

"You must be losing your tan."

"No. I've been staying at a motel with a swimming pool. Are you working, Linda? Last time we talked, you were looking for a job."

"I worked for a while in a boutique."

"What happened?"

"What happened to the job?"

"Yeah."

"I quit."

"Why?"

"I don't know. The owner wanted to make love to somebody else for a while."

"Oh."

"Fletch?"

"I'm still here. Where you left me."

"I mean. I wonder. I mean, the divorce has gone through and all. We couldn't spoil anything by being together."

"Couldn't spoil anything?"

"You know, spoil the divorce. If we had been together while the divorce was going through, you know, it might not have gone through."

"Oh. Too bad."

"Now our getting together wouldn't spoil anything."

"You want to get together?"

"I mean, it's Friday night, and I miss you, Fletch. Fletch?"

"Sure."

"Can we spend the night together?"

"Sure."

"I can be there in about an hour."

"Great. You still have a key?"

"Yes."

"I have to go out for a few minutes. There's no food in the house. I have to get some beer and some sandwich stuff."

"Okay."

"So if I'm not here when you get here, just come in and wait. I'll be back."

"All right."

"I won't be long," he said.

"You'd better be."

"Very funny. Don't bring your cat."

"I don't have a cat. See you soon, Fletch. Right after I shower."

"Yeah. Be sure and take a shower first."

"I'll see you in an hour."

After hanging up, Fletch went to the bureau, put on a fresh pair of jeans, a fresh T-shirt, grabbed his pot from the coffee table, his wallet and keys from the bookcase, turned out the lights, checked to make sure the door was locked, went down in the elevator to the garage, got into his car, and drove the hour and a half back to The Beach.

10

When he arrived, the chain light hanging from the ceiling was on. Bobbi was lying naked on the groundmat, on her back, asleep.

The room Fletch had rented at The Beach for the duration of this assignment was over a fish store. It stank.

He had furnished it with a knapsack, a bedroll, and his only luxury in that room, the groundmat.

In an ell of the room, in grossly unsanitary juxtaposition, were a two-burner stove, a tiny refrigerator which did not work well, a sink, a shower stall and a toilet.

For this room he paid a weekly rate that amounted to more per month than his city apartment. It had been rented to him by a fisherman who had the character in his face of an Andrew Wyeth subject. It was impossible to lock the door.

The noise of the pan on the stove woke Bobbi.

"Want some soup?"

She had been up, but now she was down.

"Hi."

"Hi. Want some soup?"

"Yeah. Great."

She remained inert. Her "great" had sounded a proper response to the news that pollution had killed all the rabbits on earth.

Bobbi was fifteen years old and blond. She had lost weight even in the few weeks Fletch had known her. Her knees had begun to appear too big for her legs. The skin of her small breasts had begun to wrinkle. Even with her deep tan, the skin under her eyes, almost to the base of her nose, was purple. Her cheekbones appeared to be pulling inside her head. Each eye looked as if it had been hit with a ball-peen hammer.

On her arms and legs were needle tracks.

He sat cross-legged on the mat with the pan of soup and one spoon.

"Sit up."

When she did, drawing her knees up to make room for him, her shoulders looked narrower than her ribcage.

"Been trickin'?"

"Earlier," she said.

"Make much?"

"Forty dollars. Two tricks. Nothing extra."

"Have some soup."

He tipped the spoon into her mouth.

"One guy had a great watch I tried to hook, but he didn't take his eyes off it once. The bastard."

"Did you spend the forty?"

"Yes. And used it. Now it's gone. All gone."

A childlike, ladylike tear built on the lower lid of her left eye and rolled down her cheek without her appearing to notice it.

"Cheer up. There are always more tricks tomorrow. Where did you get the stuff?"

"Fat Sam."

"Any good?"

"Sure. But he doesn't have much."

"He doesn't?"

"He said he hopes he can deal the weekend."

"Where does he get it, anyway?"

"Why?"

"I was just thinking: his source might be cheaper."

"I don't know. Somewhere on the beach, I guess."

"Did you find him on the beach?"

"Yeah. He's always there."

"He sure is."

"Where did you go, Fletch? You've been gone all day. You smell different."

"I smell different?"

"You smell more like air than like a person."

"Like air?"

"I don't know what I mean."

He said, "I was in an air-conditioned building for a while today."

"Ripping off?"

"Yeah. I was doing some lifting from a couple of stores on the Main. It takes time."

"Get much?"

"A couple of cameras. Tape recorder. Trouble is there's this store dick in one store always hassling me. Minute I show up, he eye-bugs me. I had to wait for him to go to lunch."

"It's lousy the way they always hassle you."

"Shits."

"Rip off much?"

"Twenty-three dollars' worth. Big deal."

"Not so much."

58

"Not so much."

"I mean, for all day. You were gone this morning, too."

"All fuckin' day."

"Why do they have to hassle?"

"Because they're shits. They just see you coming and they're against you. Fuck 'em."

"Fuck 'em," she said.

"Fuck 'em all. The shits."

"You know, Fletch, you could probably turn tricks."

"No."

"There are plenty of boys out."

"Kids."

"You got a better body than they have."

"Too old."

"You're only twenty-three."

"Twenty-six," he said.

"So. You could turn tricks. You'd be surprised at the men cruising."

"I've seen them."

"Sometimes they don't know which they want. A guy settled with me once, and a boy cruised by, and he said, 'Forget it,' and went off after the boy. I don't know who was more surprised—the boy, or me."

"I don't know. I don't care."

"It doesn't hurt, Fletch. Honest it doesn't."

"I suppose not."

"You might make more money, is all."

"I guess. Finish the soup."

Between her knees, she stirred the soup in the pan with the spoon, concentrating on how the soup moved.

"I mean, I was just thinking you could make more money."

"I like girls."

"So what. If someone's willing to pay, and it doesn't hurt . . ."

"Maybe I'll try it."

"Sure, you try it. You could get more. I mean, I've only seen you shoot up once or twice, Fletch."

"I can't rip off enough."

"You have this room."

"I haven't paid for it yet."

"How are you staying here?"

"The guy who owns the place fences for me. That's why I get screwed all the time."

"You give him the stuff you rip off from the stores?"

"Yeah."

"That doesn't leave much left over."

"No. Not much."

"The bastard."

"He's always hassling me for more," Fletch said.

"Not a very good arrangement," she said.

"You're from the Midwest."

"Why?"

"You sound it. You sound like you're from the Midwest. Very practical."

Bobbi said, "You don't get to have much junk."

"I pop. You know that."

"I know. But still. Pills aren't good for you. They're not natural."

"They're not biodegradable?"

"Natural substances are better. Like heroin."

"The guy I'd like to rip off," Fletch said, "is Fat Sam."

"Why?"

"All the junk he's got."

"He hasn't got much now."

"Maybe next time it comes. Next delivery. Rip off both the cash and the junk same time. That would be beautiful."

"He's a good man."

"What do you mean?"

"I mean, he's not a department store or something. He's Fat Sam. A person. He takes care of us."

"Think how much you could get if I ripped him off."

"You'll never be able to. You'll never even find his stash."

"He never seems to leave the beach. He never leaves the area of the lean-to."

"He must. To get food," Bobbi said.

"The chicks bring it to him. Wendy and Karen."

"I've brought him food."

"You have?"

"When he's asked. He gives me money and tells me what."

"Where do you get the food?"

"At the supermarket."

"You just go in and take it off the shelves?"

"Yes. How else?"

"I don't know. I'd like to rip him off. Just once. If only I could figure out where the stuff comes from."

"I don't care. It's good stuff."

"You said he's going to be having a delivery in the next few days?"

"He's got to have. He said he was short tonight, but he gave me all I could pay for. He's always been good to me."

"Did he ball you, too?"

"No. Wendy was there and Karen. I think they had just made it together."

"It would be beautiful to rip him off."

With apparent absent-mindedness, Fletch began to play with his wallet. He tossed it up in the air to catch it and a picture fell out.

Bobbi said, "Who's that?"

"Nobody."

She put the soup pan down and picked up the picture. She looked at it a long time.

"It must be somebody."

"His name's Alan Stanwyk. You've never seen him."

"Who's Alan Stanwyk?"

"Somebody I used to know. Back when I was straight. He saved my life once."

"Oh. That's why you carry his picture?"

"I've never thrown it away."

"On the back it says, 'Return to *News-Tribune* library.' "

"I ripped it off from there."

"Were you ever in the newspaper business?"

"Who, me? You must be kidding. I was in with a friend once and happened to see the picture. On a desk. I grabbed it. He saved my life once."

"How?"

"I smashed up a car. It was on fire. I was unconscious. He just happened to be passing by. He stopped and dragged me out. I understand he lives somewhere here on The Beach. Are you certain you've never seen him anywhere?"

"Absolutely certain."

"I never had a chance to say thank you."

Bobbi handed him back the picture. "I want to go to sleep now, Fletch."

"Okay."

Still sitting, he lifted off his T-shirt. When he stood up to take off his pants and turn off the light, she got into the bedroll.

He joined her.

She said, "Are you really twenty-six?"

"Yes," he lied.

"I'll never be twenty-six, will I?"

"I guess not."

"How do I feel about that?" she asked.

"I don't know."

She said, "Neither do I."

11

There are no weekends in this job, Fletch said to himself.

So on Saturday morning he got up, pulled on a pair of shorts, and went to the beach.

Creasey was there, lying on his back, elbows akimbo behind his head. At first Fletch thought he was catatonic. He may have just awakened.

The beach still had morning dew on it. Up the beach, Fat Sam's lean-to cast a long shadow.

Fletch flopped on his stomach.

"What's happening, man?"

Creasey spoke without looking at Fletch.

"Nothing much."

"Everything's cool with me," Creasey said. "Hungry. Haven't any bread for feed, have you?"

"Twelve cents." Fletch took a dime and two pennies from his pocket and tossed them on the sand near Creasey.

Creasey snorted. He was not impressed by the dime and two cents.

"You must be one of the world's greatest rip-off artists," Creasey said.

"The shitty store dicks know me now."

"You gotta go farther afield, man. Hitch rides to neighboring towns."

"How do I get stuff back to fence?"

"Motorists are very obliging. They'll pick up a man with three portable television sets any day."

Creasey laughed by rolling down his lower lip and puffing air from his diaphragm through rotten teeth.

"I used to be a pretty good house burglar myself," Creasey said. "I even had equipment."

"What happened?"

"I got ripped off. Some bastard stole my burglary equipment. The bastard."

"That's funny."

"A fuckin' riot."

"You should have had business insurance."

"I haven't got the energy now anyway." Creasey imitated a stretch and put the back of his head on the sand. "I'm gettin' old, man."

"You must be takin' the wrong stuff."

"Good stuff. Last night was glory road all the way."

Originally, Creasey had been a drummer in a rock band. They made it big. A big New York record company invested one hundred thousand dollars in them and profited three and a half million dollars from them in one year. They made a record, went on a national promotion tour, made another record, went on a national concert tour, made a third record and followed an international concert tour with another national tour. Creasey kept up, with the drumming, the traveling, the hassling with drugs, liquor and groupies. After the year he had six thousand dollars of his own and less energy than a turnip. The record company replaced him in the band with a kid from Arkansas. Creasey was grateful; he never wanted to work again.

"I used to rip off houses all over The Beach. Even up into The Hills. Beautiful, man. I hit the house of one poor son of a bitch seven times. Every time I ripped him off, he'd go out and buy the same shit. Even the same brands. RCA stereo, a Sony TV, a Nikon camera. And leave them in the same places. It was almost a game we had. He'd buy them and leave them around his house for me, and I'd rip them off. Beautiful. The eighth time I went, the house was bare-ass empty. He had stolen himself and his possessions away. An extreme man."

"No more energy for that, uh?"

"Nah, man; that was work. I might as well be beatin' my brains out on a set."

"Where's the bread goin' to come from now?"

"I don't know, man. I don't care."

"Fat Sam must be paid."

"He must," Creasey said. "Son of a bitch."

Fletch said, "I wonder where he gets the stuff."

Creasey answered, "I wouldn't know about that."

"I'm not asking," Fletch said.

"I know you're not. I'd rip him off in a minute. That way, I'd have my own supply. And he could always get more. But the son of a bitch never leaves the beach. At least not while I'm aware. Can't figure the son of a bitch out."

The last time there had been a panic, when there had been an extraordinary number of junkies around and Fat Sam had declared himself absolutely clean, out of everything, at night, Fletch had sat up the beach in the moonlight and watched the lean-to all night. No one came or went from Fat Sam's lean-to. Fletch spoke with anyone who came near. They were all frantic, desperate people. None of them had a supply.

By eleven-thirty the next morning, word went out that Fat Sam—

without leaving his lean-to—was fully supplied again. And he was. The panic was over.

"He's a magician," Creasey said. "A fuckin' magician."

"He must be. Bobbi says he's short now."

"Yeah. Rationing's on this day. Ah, me. Not to worry. He'll get the stuff. I mean, I'm sure he'll get the stuff. Don't you think he'll get the stuff? I mean, plenty of it? Like, he always has. I mean, you know, he always gets the stuff. In time. Sometimes he's short for a day or two, and there's rationing, you know, but he always gets the stuff. He'll get it this time, too."

"I'm sure he'll get it," Fletch said.

"He'll get it."

"I'm sure of it," Fletch said.

"Hey, Fletch. You ever notice the way the same kid is always busted?"

"Yeah."

"Man, that's funny. Always the same kid."

"He's a local kid. Montgomery?"

"Gummy Montgomery."

"His dad's a big cheese in the town."

"Every ten days, two weeks, they pick him up. Question him. Beat the shit out of him all night. Let him go in the morning. In the morning, he's back at Fat Sam's for more."

"I guess he never talks."

"He couldn't. We'd all be cooled if he ever did. Oh, man, the fuzz are stupid."

"They only care about the locals. Montgomery's father is superintendent of schools or something."

"Questioning begins at home. They know none of us would ever talk. So they always pick him up, the same kid, and beat the shit out of him. Funny, funny."

"You have a great sense of humor this morning, Creasey."

"I had a beautiful night. The stars came down and talked to me."

"What did they say?"

"They said, 'Creasey, you are the chosen of God. You are chosen to lead the people into the sea.' "

"A wet dream."

"Yeah. A wet dream."

"I've got to go see the man about some horse," Fletch said.

"I gotta go steal some bread."

Creasey did not move. He remained staring into the sea where he would lead the people on his next high.

Fletch sat cross-legged in the shade of Vatsyayana's lean-to. Vatsyayana was sitting cross-legged inside the lean-to.

"Peace," Vatsyayana said.

"Fuck," said Fletch.

"That, too."

"Some reds," Fletch said.

"I'm fresh out."

"I've got twenty dollars."

"Expecting a shipment any day. Hang in there."

"Need it now."

"I understand." Vatsyayana had the world's kindliest eyes. "No got. I've got what's left of the horse."

"Horseshit."

"Each to his own taste. How's Bobbi?"

"Asleep."

"She really grooves on you, Fletch. She was here last night."

"I know. You didn't ball her."

"Who could? By the time she shows up here, she's had it. Did you ball her last night?"

"No."

"She looks terrible, Fletch."

"Thank you."

"I mean it, Fletch."

"I know. I think she has fetuses going on all the time."

"That's not possible."

"No. She's not strong enough to carry anything."

"Why don't you get her away from here?"

"You think Gummy will talk?"

From the back of the lean-to, Vatsyayana's eyes momentarily brightened. "I don't think so."

66

"Why not? They keep beatin' on him."

"He hasn't talked yet."

"Why do they keep pickin' on the same kid?"

"He's local. They can put more pressure on him. I guess they figure if they keep hammerin' on the same kid, instead of hammerin' on you one day and me the next, over time they can break him down and get him to turn state's evidence. I've seen it before."

"Will it work? I mean, will they break him down?"

"I doubt it. He's in very deep now. He feels nothing."

"How will we know if he talks?"

"The men in blue with big sticks will come swooping down out of the skies, Society's avenging angels, sunlight glistening from their riot helmets."

"How will we know it's going to happen?"

"It won't happen. Believe me, Fletch. You're all right. It won't happen."

"Fat Sam, I heard someone say he wanted to rip you off."

"Who?"

"I won't say."

"Creasey? These days, Creasey can hardly walk so far."

"Not Creasey. Someone else."

"Who'd want to rip off Vatsyayana?"

"He says he even knows your source."

"No one knows Vatsyayana's source."

"He says he does. He says you get your delivery here on the beach. That someone brings it to you. Is that true?"

"Son, there is no truth."

"He says the next time you get delivery he's gonna be there. He's got some scheme where he picks up both the cash and the junk."

"Not possible. It doesn't work that way."

"What way?"

"It doesn't work any way."

"How do you get it?"

"I pray for it and it comes. You're a good boy, Fletch, but you're not too bright. Has anyone ever told you that before?"

"Yes."

"I bet they have. No one's gonna rip off Vatsyayana."

"Is it possible? I mean, you could be ripped off."

"No way. Not possible. Just relax. By tomorrow noon I should have some reds. Can you make it?"

"Gimme the H."

"Gimme the twenty."

"No one would want you ripped off, Sam."

"If it ever happened, it would be bye-bye highs."

"No one would want that to happen."

"Of course not."

"The Stanwyk residence."

Fletch had turned on the fan in the roof of the telephone booth to dampen the sound of traffic.

"Mrs. Stanwyk, please."

"I'm sorry, Mrs. Stanwyk isn't in. May I take a message?"

"We're calling from the Racquets Club. Do you have any idea where Mrs. Stanwyk is?"

"Why, she should be there, sir, at the club. She was playing this morning, and she said she would be staying for lunch. I think she's meeting her father there."

"Ah, then she's here now?"

"Yes, sir. She planned to spend most of the day at the club."

"We'll have a look for her. Sorry to bother you."

Saturday morning traffic at The Beach was heavy. Down the street was a department store.

Fletch bought a new T-shirt, a pair of white socks, and a pair of tennis shorts.

12

"You're Joan Stanwyk, aren't you?"

She was sitting alone at a table for two overlooking the tennis courts. A half-empty martini on the rocks was in front of her.

"Why, yes."

"I haven't seen you since your wedding."

"Are you a friend of Alan's?"

"We were in the Air Force together," Fletch said. "In San Antonio. I haven't seen Alan in years."

"You're very clever to have recognized me."

"How could I forget? May I sit down?"

Fletch had left his car in the club parking lot and had gone around the building past the kitchen door to the service entrance to the locker rooms. The freshest sign on a locker door said Underwood. A new member. They and their guests could not yet be well known to the club staff.

When he had come onto the tennis pavilion, the headwaiter had said, "Pardon me, sir. Are you a guest of the club?"

Fletch had answered, "I'm a guest of the Underwoods."

"They're not here, sir. I haven't seen them."

"They're coming later."

"Very good, sir. Perhaps you'd like a drink while you're waiting?"

Fletch had spotted Joan Stanwyk.

"We'll put it on the Underwood bill."

"A screwdriver, please."

He sat at Joan Stanwyk's table.

"I'm afraid my memory isn't so good, although it should be," Joan Stanwyk said. "I can't remember your name."

"No one can," Fletch said. "The world's most forgettable name. Utrelamensky. John Utrelamensky."

"John I can remember."

On the table was a Polaroid camera.

"Are you from this area, John?"

"No. Butte, Montana. I'm here on business. In fact, I'm leaving on a midafternoon plane."

"And what business would that be?"

"Furniture. We sell to hotels, that sort of thing."

"I see. Too bad you won't be able to see Alan. He's at a flying convention in Idaho."

"Alan still flying?"

"Relentlessly."

"Unlike some of the rest of us, he really enjoyed it. I'll never forget the time he buzzed a house in San Antonio with a training jet."

"He buzzed a house?"

"He never told you? Shattered glass. The police were out after him. He was severely reprimanded for it."

"Funny the things husbands don't tell you."

"I expect he's not too proud of it."

"How nice to meet an old friend of Alan's. I mean, meet again. Tell me more."

"Only wrong thing I ever knew of him doing. We weren't that close, anyway. I just happened to be out here the week of the wedding, bumped into him and he said, 'Come along.'"

"But surely you're a good deal younger than my husband?"

"Not much," Fletch said. "I'm thirty."

"You look young for your age."

"The furniture business has been good to me."

"Well, I'm sure Alan will be sorry to have missed you."

"I'm not so sure."

"Oh?"

"We had a political difference at your reception."

"About what?"

"I made some crack about big business. Alan didn't like it a bit."

"How could you?" There was mockery in her eyes.

"I was younger then. I had not yet received a corporate paycheck."

"Did you say anything about his marrying the boss's daughter?"

"No. Is that what he did?"

"He married the boss's daughter—me. He's a bit sensitive about that. That's probably why he got so angry."

"I see. I hadn't realized that. I guess I really goofed."

"Never mind. He's been accused of it enough times. Poor Alan spends all his available time proving he married me for myself and not for Poppa's business."

"He works for your father?"

"I'm not sure at the moment who works for whom. Alan runs the place. Dad runs tennis tournaments. In fact, these days Dad does pretty much what Alan tells him."

70

"Alan always was very competent."

"Remarkably."

"What sort of a business is this, anyway?"

"Collins Aviation."

"I never heard of it. Sorry."

"You wouldn't have, unless you were in the aviation business. It makes parts for airplanes the actual airplane manufacturers put together."

"Not exactly a dry-cleaning shop."

"Not exactly."

"You see how bad I am at business. I don't even follow the stock market."

"Very little of Collins Aviation stock is available. It belongs mostly to us."

"The whole thing?"

"To us and a few family friends. You know, like the family doctor, Dad's old Harvard roommate, Joe Devlin . . . people like that. All as rich as Croesus."

"How nice."

"It is nice to have everyone you know rich. Problems never come up about who pays the drink bill."

"Would you like another?"

"Why, John. How nice." He signaled a waiter.

"By the way, John, how did you gain entrée to the Racquets Club?"

"I'm a guest of the Underwoods. He and I are doing a little business together. He knew my plane was not leaving until midafternoon, so he suggested I come over, hit a ball and have a swim."

"The Underwoods? I don't know them. They must be new members."

"I'm sure I wouldn't know."

"But where's your tennis racquet?"

"I borrowed one. I just returned it to the pro shop."

"I see."

"A martini on the rocks, please, and a screwdriver," he said.

The waiter said, "Yes, Mrs. Stanwyk."

"The Racquets Club is Daddy's pet. He darn near built the place himself. In fact, he's endowed it so well, the Racquets Club is a major stockholder in Collins Aviation. That very chair you're sitting on was probably designed for an airport lounge in Albany. Does Albany have an airport?"

"Albany, New York?"

"Yes."

"Who cares?"

"Good point. Who cares about Albany, New York?"

"Except the Albanians."

"Except the Albanians. Woo. I usually don't drink martinis after playing tennis in the morning."

"What do you usually do after playing tennis in the morning?"

"I wouldn't mind doing that either," she said. "Alan's away a lot. Mondays and Wednesdays he never gets home before eleven o'clock at night. The ends of the weeks he's apt to get in his airplane and go somewhere on business. Business, business, business. Ah, here's another drink."

The waiter said, "Here you are, Mrs. Stanwyk."

"To business," she said.

"He never comes home until eleven on Mondays and Wednesdays?" Fletch repeated.

"Very late. On Thursdays I have a committee meeting here at the club. Just as well; the servants at home are out. Julie and I have supper here at the Club. Julie's my daughter. You haven't met her yet. I don't know what happens to Alan on Thursdays. That leaves us exactly Tuesdays together. He's always very attentive on Tuesdays."

"I remember Alan got a piece of metal stuck in him overseas."

"He got a scar in his belly and a Purple Heart."

"Is he all right now?"

"Perfect. He's in perfect physical condition."

"He is?"

"Why are you so incredulous?"

"He always worried about having cancer. Every time he lit a cigarette he'd mention it. He called them cancer sticks."

"I have noted no such justifiable neuroticism on his part."

72

"He's never had cancer?"

"God. Don't even say it."

"Remarkable."

"What is?"

"That he's never had cancer."

"He doesn't smoke all that much. But for you, John whatever-your-last-name-is, there seems nothing wrong with you."

"I never went overseas," Fletch said.

"You seem quite perfect."

"Overflight."

"What?"

"Overflight. I'm trying to think of the name of Alan's best man. Over-something."

"Eberhart. Burt Eberhart."

"That's it. He struck me as a nice guy. Is he still around?"

"You have some memory. He's still around. Fat and balding. He lives here on The Beach, on Vizzard Road. Married to a social climber. Three ugly kids. He's in the insurance business."

"The insurance business?"

"Yes. He handles Alan's insurance, and now the company's insurance, and the club's. He has been well set up. By Alan. They were friends at Colgate."

"Sounds like a good business. Seeing Alan's still flying, he's probably got a lot of insurance on him."

"A foolish amount. My father wanted to teach Alan, via the route of monthly premiums paid by Alan himself, the value of Alan's precious life. An effort to get him to stop flying after Julie was born. It worked not at all. Alan remains perfectly willing to cast his wife and child to the insurance adjuster just to climb through the clouds to sudden sunlight once again."

"Alan pays the premiums? Not the company?"

"When we say 'the company' in my family, we mean my father. Dad obliges Alan to have such insurance coverage as a condition of his employment, but Alan must pay the bill himself. Daddy's very cute at making such arrangements. Pity they never work."

"I should think, from what you say, Alan would need to get away and have some fun by himself once in a while."

"There's the club."

"He relaxes when he flies," he said.

"And everyone else has heart failure. I hate to think what he's flying this weekend. For fun. You wouldn't even recognize those experimental craft he flies as airplanes. They look like the mean, nasty sort of weapons aborigines throw through the air. Horrifying."

"It must be tough on you."

"I wish he'd stop flying."

"One thing I've always wondered about."

"Dad is late for lunch."

"Is he coming?"

"He was supposed to meet me here twenty minutes ago."

"Perhaps I should leave."

"No, no. He'd be happy to meet you. Any friend of Alan's and all that. What were you wondering about?"

"Why Alan's parents didn't come to the wedding."

"Alan's parents?"

"Yes."

"They're estranged. He never sees them."

"He never sees them?"

"Does that surprise you?"

"Yes, it does. I had the idea they were rather close."

"No way. He hates them. Alan always has. I've never even met them."

"How can that be so?"

"You must be thinking of someone else."

"I'm sure Alan used to fly home to see his parents whenever he could. Every six weeks or so."

"Not Alan. His parents were very pushy toward him. The crisis came, I think, at the Golden Gloves."

"The Golden Gloves? I remember Alan had boxed."

"Alan boxed because his father made him. Pushed him right up the ladder or whatever into the state Golden Gloves. When he was fifteen. Every day after school he had to spend in the basement at home, boxing until supper time. He hated it. He refused to go into the nationals. He and his father have never spoken since then."

"I must be confused."

"You must be. And he's always said his mother is a sickly, neurotic thing. Spends most of her time in bed."

"Aren't you interested in these people? Alan's parents? Aren't you curious to meet them yourself?"

"Not if what Alan says is true about them. And I'm sure it is. Why wouldn't it be? Believe me, honey, I have enough difficult people around me to not want to add in-laws."

"I see."

There was a stir in the pavilion as a handsome, distinguished-looking man in his fifties entered, dressed in white tennis slacks and blue blazer. People reacted like children in a sandbox catching sight of someone coming with a box of popsicles. They waved from their tables. Men nearest the entrance stood up to shake hands. Women beamed. The headwaiter welcomed with happy bows of his head.

"There," Joan said, "is Dad."

Fletch said, "Yes, I remember him."

"Don't be disappointed if he doesn't remember you."

"Why should he remember me?" Fletch said.

"Because you're beautiful," she said. "You really turn me on. Are you sure you have to leave town today?"

"I've got to be back tonight."

"But tomorrow's Sunday."

"Listen," Fletch said, "you and Alan ought to have a place you can go and be by yourselves once in a while. I mean, a place of your own."

"The ranch."

"What?"

"Alan is buying a ranch. In Nevada. For us."

"Great."

"No, it isn't great. It's awful. Who wants a ranch in Nevada?"

"Most people."

"I spent a summer on a ranch when I was a kid. Hot, dusty, dirty. Boring. Incredibly boring. All the men look like pretzels. And when

they talk they sound like a Dick-and-Jane book. It comes out slow
and it ends up obvious. And you don't talk about anything that hasn't
got four legs. I mean, sitting around looking at a cow is not my idea
of pleasure."

"Then why are you doing it?"

"Alan wants to. He thinks the ranch is a great idea as an investment. I haven't even been out to look at it. He insists he's taking
me next weekend."

"Next weekend?"

"I can't tell you how I'm looking forward to it."

"It's a place you could be alone together."

"Like hell. There's an airstrip in the back yard. I know that already.
As long as there's an airplane in the back yard, Alan will be off on
an important business deal somewhere and I'll be left staring at cows
with a bunch of pretzels in blue jeans."

"So stop it. Stop Alan from buying it."

"Supposedly, he's taking the down payment, the cash, out himself
next weekend."

"The cash? As cash?"

"Yes. Isn't that crazy? Cash. He said cash, visible cash is the only
way to do business with these people. If he shows up with cash in
a brown paper bag or something, flashes the real stuff, he might save
percentages from the purchase price."

"They must be more sophisticated than that."

"This is deep in Nevada, honey. How do you know what appeals
to a pretzel in blue jeans with a cow on its mind? Oh, Dad."

Fletch stood up.

"This is an old friend of Alan's. They were in the Air Force
together. John—"

Shaking hands, Fletch said, "Yahmenaraleski."

"Glad to meet you, Mr. Yahmenaraleski," John Collins said. "Stay
and have lunch with us."

13

Fletch brought a chair from a neighboring table and sat in it. John Collins sat facing his daughter. At one o'clock, the sunlit tennis courts were empty. The pavilion was full.

Joan had moved the Polaroid camera.

"John's in the furniture business, Dad. From Grand Rapids, Michigan."

"From Butte, Montana," Fletch said.

"Oh?"

Fletch was correct. Besides no one's being able to remember for long the name he gave, no one cared to inquire too deeply into either the furniture business or Butte, Montana. He believed himself absolutely unmemorable.

"Martinis before lunch?" John Collins said.

"I mean to take a nap this afternoon." Joan stared at Fletch.

"I'm glad to see at least John is drinking orange juice."

"It's a screwdriver."

"Ah. Well. If you drink enough of those, they'll make your head hammer." John Collins beamed at them both. His daughter groaned softly. "You play tennis, John?"

"Just hack about, sir. I enjoy the game, but I have so little time for it . . ."

"You must make time in life to enjoy yourself and be healthy. It's the best way to get a lot done."

"Yes, sir."

"Of course it also helps if you have a very able son-in-law to take over your business and run it for you. Sometimes I feel guilty that I'm playing and Alan is working. How do you know Alan?"

"We were in the Air Force together. In Texas."

"John said that Alan buzzed a house once, in San Antonio. Did he ever mention that to you, Dad?"

"He certainly didn't."

"We were lieutenants then," Fletch said. "He was severely reprimanded. I guess I talked out of school."

"Delighted you did," John Collins said. "Time we had a bit of dirt on Alan. I'll put his nose in it. Got any more dirt?"

"No, sir."

"He's off flying someone's idea of an airplane in Idaho this weekend," John said. "Do you still fly?"

"Only with a ticket in my hand."

"Good for you. I wish Alan would give it up. He's too important to too many people to be taking such risks. Were you overseas with him?"

"No, sir. I was sent to the Aleutians."

"Oh."

Fletch smiled. No one cared about the Aleutians, either.

Without having ordered, John Collins was brought a grilled cheese sandwich and a bottle of ale.

"Aren't you two going to order?" he asked.

"Sliced chicken sandwich," Joan said. "Mayonnaise."

"A grilled cheese," Fletch added. "Bottle of Coors beer."

"How very ingratiating of you," John Collins said.

He was used to young men complimenting him over his choice of lunch.

Fletch laughed. "I'm very happy in the furniture business, thank you."

"Actually, Alan needs more young men around him. Friends. People he can trust. He's stuck with all my old office cronies. I keep telling him he should retire them all off, but he's too smart for that. He says he would rather have attrition than contrition."

"Dad. He never said anything of the sort."

"Well, he would have, if he had a sense of humor."

"He has a lovely sense of humor," Joan said.

"Tell me something he ever said that made you laugh," John said. "Anything."

"Well. He said something to Julie the other day. But I can't remember it. Something about going to bed."

78

"A riot," John said. "My son-in-law is a riot. Did he have a sense of humor when you knew him in Texas?"

"A pretty serious fellow," Fletch said.

"I worry about people who don't have a sense of humor. Here's your lunch. Take everything seriously. They're apt to kill themselves."

"If the cigarettes don't get them first," Fletch said.

"What?" John Collins leaned on him.

"The cigarettes. Alan was always dreadfully afraid of cancer."

"He should be. No one should smoke."

Joan said, "Alan's never mentioned his fear of cancer to me."

"He must be used to it," Fletch said. "Or over it."

"Everybody should be afraid of cancer. Does it run in his family? Of course, how do we know? Never met his family. Ought to look them up and see if they're still alive."

"Alan never speaks of them," Joan said. "I doubt he even hears from them."

"I don't blame him. Any man who makes his son box is a jackass. A stupid sport. Alan would have been a great tennis player if he had started young and not been forced to waste all his time getting bopped on the nose. Rather, I should say, any man who forces his son to box wants to see him in a coffin."

"You're in top form today, Dad. One right after the other."

"Why not? Pleasant company. His father just never realized what an intelligent lad Alan was and is. Wonder he didn't get his brains knocked out of him."

"Before you came, Dad, we were talking about the damn-fool ranch Alan is buying, in Nevada."

"Yes. Good idea."

"It's a terrible idea."

"This family doesn't have anywhere near enough invested in real estate. And what there is is downtown space. Or the place in Aspen, whatnot. We should be much more heavily invested in land. No one's ever wanted to manage it. I'm glad Alan does."

Joan said, "I hate the whole idea."

"You don't have to go there."

"The way Alan talks, a million acres in Nevada is going to be our spiritual home."

"You'll have to go there once in a while, of course, while Alan goes over things. Do you both good to get away. With Julie. You must be sick to death of your mother and me living on top of you."

"She's not well."

John said, "I remember the first day I saw your mother taking martinis before lunch. Gin is a depressant, my girl."

"My golly. You do live on top of us. I never noticed before."

"Was Jim Swarthout helpful?" John asked.

"Who?"

"Jim Swarthout of Swarthout Nevada Realty. Biggest firm in Nevada. I sent Alan to him when he began talking about the ranch. I understood he's been dealing with him."

"Oh, yes. Very helpful. He's the man who found the ranch for Alan. He's mentioned him several times. He is the real estate broker. We're going down next weekend, cash in hand."

"Cheer up, old girl. Alan's dead right about our investing in a ranch. He couldn't be more right." John Collins drained his ale. "Now the job is to see if we can get young John here a tennis match."

"No, sir. Thank you anyway. I haven't the time, at this point. My plane leaves midafternoon."

"Oh." The man seemed genuinely disappointed. "I'm sorry to hear that."

"This is a beautiful club, though. Joan mentioned the extent of your contribution to it."

"Well, she shouldn't have. But I consider it very important. Young people have to have a place to go, and healthy things to do. You know, I understand young people can't even go to the beach here anymore."

"Oh?"

"Drugs. Goddamn it. Drugs everywhere. On the beach, of all places. Hard drugs. Heroin. Opium. Let alone these pills and amphetamines. Sending a youngster to the beach these days is equal to sending him to hell."

"People literally selling drugs to children. Pushing drugs on them. Can you imagine anything worse than that?" Joan said. "What sort of an insane, evil person would actually urge children to take drugs for just a few bucks?"

"I've had several conversations with the chief of police, Chief Cummings," John Collins said, "urging him to crack down more actively on this business. I've even offered to pay to have special investigators come in, to clean the whole thing up. That's a bill I wouldn't mind paying at all. He tells me he's doing everything he can. He has an informer on the beach, he says, but it's very difficult, as young people drift in and out, live on the beach, go by phony names. Apparently it's much too fluid a situation to control. There are no constants. He said special investigators wouldn't do a darn bit of good."

"I didn't know you made that offer, Dad. How sweet."

"It's not sweet. It's necessary. With the rate of burglaries we're having here at The Beach, muggings and robberies, something has to be done. There's going to be a murder soon, and then people will sit up. But what really bothers me is all these young people staggering around, destroying their brains, destroying their bodies, killing themselves. How very awful for them. They don't know better. Their lives must be just hell."

Fletch said, "I quite agree with you, sir."

"However, the esteemed chief of police is retiring soon, and a man close to retirement isn't apt to be at his most energetic. That's what I keep telling Alan: retire the old farts; give them their money and let them go. They're not doing anything for the company anyway. Chief Cummings is busy setting up some retirement home. He's not paying attention to police business here in town. Might as well get rid of him. Perhaps after he retires, we'll have a better chance to wipe out this nest of vipers and sickies."

Fletch said,"You never can tell. The thing might break by itself, somehow."

"I'd like to see it," John Collins said. "And I'd like to know who is going to do it."

"Well," Fletch said. "The club is just great."

"There are no drugs here," John Collins said, "except for martinis imbibed before lunch by certain dopes."

14

Using his telephone credit card, Fletch spent an hour in an over-stuffed chair in the playroom of the Racquets Club. The room was dark and cool, and no one was at the billiard tables or the ping-pong tables or watching the television.

First, he called the home number of Marvin Stanwyk in Nonheagan, Pennsylvania.

"Mr. Stanwyk?"

"Yes."

"This is Sidney James of Casewell Insurers of California."

"How are you, boy? What did you decide about picking up that Bronze Star?"

"I haven't decided yet, sir."

"Doubt you'll ever be offered another one."

"I didn't expect to be offered this one."

"I say you should pick it up. Never know. You might have a son, someday, who'd have some interest in it, or a grandson."

"I don't know, sir. Women don't seem to be having children these days."

"You know, you're right about that. I wouldn't mind Alan and his wife producing a child."

"What?"

"Don't you think it's time they had a child? Been married how long? Six, seven years?"

"They don't have a child?"

"Indeed not. That would get us to come out to California. Boy, girl, anything. We wouldn't miss seeing our grandchild."

"I see."

"Well, Mr. James, I imagine you called to ask how we are again. Mrs. Stanwyk and I are both well. Just beginning to think about lunch."

"Glad to hear it, sir."

"You must be a pretty ambitious fellow, working on a Saturday. I have to go back to the hardware store myself after lunch, but I thought I was the only man left alive who still works on a Saturday. Of course, in your case, you may have to work on Saturday because you spend so much time the rest of the week calling up people."

"We're trying to pin down just how much flying your son does."

"Too much."

"You say he comes to see you every six weeks or so."

"About that."

"How long does he stay with you?"

"A night or two."

"Does he stay in your house?"

"No. He and the copilot or whatever he is stay at the Nonheagan Inn. They have a suite there. Alan's like you. If he's not on the phone forty-five minutes an hour, he thinks the world's going to end. He needs the hotel switchboard."

"How much do you actually see him on a visit?"

"I'm not sure I'll ever get used to your questions, but a man who won the Bronze Star must know what he's doin'. Mostly they come for breakfast."

"They?"

"He and the copilot. Name is Bucky. That's why my wife always makes him buckwheat cakes. He loves them. He can put away more buckwheat cakes than you need to shingle your roof."

"Is it always the same pilot?"

"No. Twice it's been other fellows, but I don't remember their names. Usually it's Bucky. Then, sometimes, Alan might come over by himself later, for supper. Not always. We don't see that much of him when he's here, but we guess he just finds his old hometown restful."

"Yes, of course. How long has he been doing this?"

"Visiting us regularly? Since he became the big cheese out at that airplane company. I guess business brings him east more now."

"The last six or seven years?"

"I'd say the last four years. We saw him hardly at all when he was first married. Which is apt to be the way."

"Why do you say he flies too much?"

"Flying's dangerous, son. Especially in a private jet. Anything could go wrong."

"You mean he could get hurt."

"He could get killed. I haven't heard they're making airplanes out of rubber yet. He's already been in one air crash, you know. Two, in fact. Overseas."

"I know. You didn't mind his boxing, though, when he was a kid."

"Who says we didn't?"

"You did mind?"

"We did about everything we could think of to make him stop. Every afternoon down there in the cellar beating the beeswax out of the punching bags. Whump, whump, whump. Till supper time. There was a period when he was out fighting two nights a week. No one's brain can stand that. I was sure his brain was going to run out his ears. Enough ran out his nose."

"Why didn't you stop him from boxing, then?"

"If you ever have a son, you'll find that when he gets to be fourteen or fifteen there are some things you can't tell him not to do. The more you tell them not to smash their heads against the wall, the more they insist upon doing it. They never believe they're going to need things like brains later on in life."

"Then why didn't he go on to the nationals?"

"You can't figure the answer to that question?"

"No, sir."

"Girls, son; girls. No matter how much time fifteen-year-old boys spend thrashing around in the basement, sooner or later they notice girls. And that's the end of their thrashing around in the basement. The boxing gloves were hung up and out came the pocket comb. I admit, though, it took us a while to figure it out. He had sure wanted to go to the nationals, and he was very, very good at out-boxing people. Suddenly, before the nationals, the house stopped shaking, the whumping ceased. We thought he was sick. The night he told us he was not going to the nationals was about the happiest night of our lives. The punching bags are still hanging in our basement. Never touched them since. They need a rest after the beating they took. Then, of course, Alan took to flying airplanes. Sons just don't know how to keep their parents relaxed. I'm sure you weren't a bit kinder to your parents, Mr. James."

"I guess not. Maybe it's just as well your son and daughter-in-law don't have a child."

"Aw, no. Bringing up kids is not the same as eating creamed chicken, but you shouldn't miss it."

"Well, I guess that's all for now, Mr. Stanwyk. Thanks again."

"Say, son?"

"Yes?"

"I'm glad you called back, because I didn't know where to reach you. I've been thinking about your Bronze Star. I want to make a deal with you."

"Oh?"

"Well, you ought to pick it up. What I'm thinking is this. You pick the Bronze Star up and send it out to us. We'll admire it and hold it for you, and someday when you want it, when you have a kid or something, we'll send it back to you."

"That's very nice of you."

"What do you say? If anything happens to us, we'll make sure you get it somehow. We'll leave it with the bank along with my wife's best shoes."

"I don't know what to say."

"It's a long life, son, and your feelings change about things. You send the Bronze Star on to us, and we'll take care of it for you."

"You're a sweet man, Mr. Stanwyk."

"I don't understand that California kind of talk."

"May I think about it?"

"Sure. I'm just thinking it might make the whole thing easier for you."

"Thank you. Thank you very much."

"Call anytime. I bought some more telephone stock last night."

"The Nonheagan Inn. Good afternoon."

"Good afternoon. This is Mr. Alan Stanwyk."

"Hello, Mr. Stanwyk. Nice to hear your voice, sir."

Teenage girls looked into the Racquets Club playroom. Apparently Fletch was not what they were looking for.

"I'm calling myself because it's Saturday and I just decided I might come out next weekend."

"Oh?"

"Why does that surprise you?"

"Sorry, sir. I didn't mean to sound surprised. It's just that we look forward to seeing you every six weeks or so, and you were here just two weeks ago."

"I may change my mind about coming."

"It will be perfectly all right if you do, sir. We'll keep the suite for you until we're sure you're not coming."

"Thank you very much."

"Good-bye, Mr. Stanwyk."

"Swarthout Nevada Realty Company."

"Jim Swarthout, please."

"I'm sorry, sir, Mr. Swarthout is out with a client."

"When do you expect him?"

"Well, sir, it is Saturday afternoon . . ."

"I see."

"May I have him call you after he calls in?"

"No, thanks. He'll be in the office Monday?"

"Yes, sir."

"I'll get him then."

15

Still in tennis whites, Fletch cruised slowly down Vizzard Road. The telephone directory had said the number was 12355.

It was a pleasant Spanish-styled stucco house set back on a cool lawn. In the driveway was a blue Cadillac Coupe de Ville.

Fletch parked in the street.

Going toward the house, he smelled and saw smoke, so he went around to the back.

Inside the pool enclosure was a fat, balding man in Bermuda shorts contemplating a lighted hibachi. Beside him on a flagstone was a large gin and tonic.

"Burt?"

The man looked up, ready to be pleased, ready to greet someone, to be glad; instead, he looked slightly hesitant at someone he had never seen before.

"John Zalumarinero," Fletch said.

"Oh, yes."

Burt Eberhart put out his hand.

"I'm only in town for the day. Just had lunch with Joan Collins and her father at the Racquets Club."

"Oh, yes."

"I asked for you. Joan said you lived here at The Beach and I should pop in to say hello on the way back to the hotel."

"Oh, yes."

"I haven't seen you since Joan's wedding. You were best man."

"John!" Burt Eberhart said with a burst of synthetic recognition. He shook hands again. "By God, it's good to see you again. How have you been keeping yourself?"

"Furniture business. Montana."

"That's terrific. You look so young. You say you just had lunch with Joan and her dad?"

"The grilled cheese special."

"Jesus. John Collins and his grilled cheese sandwich. A billionaire practically, and he gives you a grilled cheese sandwich. I'd hate to see what he'd eat if he were poor. I know what you mean, fella. I've had plenty of his grilled cheese sandwiches. At least he could buy you a steak. With his money. He's afraid of putting on a pound. As if anybody cares. Everybody's too busy weighing John's wallet to care what he looks like."

"You look prosperous enough yourself."

"Now no cracks, boy. What can I get you to drink? A gin and tonic?"

"That would be fine."

"It's right here, right here." A bar was in the shade, against the house. "Never be more than ten feet away from your next drink, I always say."

And he looked it.

"We had great fun at the wedding together, you and I," Fletch said. "I guess you don't remember."

"God, I was bombed out of my mind. I don't remember anything. For all I know, I was the one who got married that day. What did you say your last name is again?"

"Zalumarinero."

"That's right, that's right. An Irish boy."

"Welsh, actually."

"I remember now. We did have fun. Wasn't that a beautiful wedding? Oh, God, did we have fun. I remember you: you went right into the pool with your hat on."

"I did?"

"You did. You certainly did. You walked right up to the pool with your hat on and kept right on walking. Splash! Any man who can do a thing like that can't be all bad."

"I don't remember."

"I wasn't the only one putting them down that day, my boy. Here's to your health. Oh, God, it's hot. Why people live in this climate I'll never know. We all rush to California because of the beautiful climate, and then spend the rest of our lives indoors hugging an air-conditioner. Come sit by the hibachi. We're having a few people over later."

Fletch sat in the shade of an umbrella and watched Burt fiddle with the hibachi between gulps of his drink.

"The trick to a good charcoaled steak is to start the fire plenty early. Two or three hours ahead of time. Our ancestors, you know, used to have the fire going all the time. Of course they weren't paying what we are for charcoal. Then, when they wanted to use the fire, it would be right there, ready, and they could control it. You can't control a new fire as well. Golly, I'm awful glad you stopped by, John. You should stay for supper."

"No, thanks, I really can't."

"I mean, you should. Anybody who has lunch with John Collins needs a steak supper. And a battle ribbon."

"My plane leaves in a couple of hours."

"Then you should have another drink. I always believe in being at least as high as the plane. That way, if it falls down, you still have a chance."

"How's Alan?"

"Oh, he's terrific. Beautiful. He looks like you. Not an inch of fat on his body. Great shape, great shape. Just watching him makes me tired."

"I think you said at the wedding you and he were great friends at school."

"Colgate, ta-ra! I've been living off him ever since."

"What do you mean?"

"Almost ever since. I had a few lean years before he got married. I had to work for a living. Want another drink? I've got all his insurance accounts. His life insurance, house, cars, inland marine, the Collins Company. That's why I never disagree with John Collins, despite the grilled cheese sandwiches. After all, I've got my future drinking to consider."

"Joan said Alan's life is insured for three million dollars."

"You'd better believe it."

"It's true?"

"Absolutely true. That guy's worth a lot more dead than alive. Except to me. I get the premiums commission. Every night I pray for him. If he dies, I die. I'd even have to go back to work. Jesus. Think of it. Some damn-ass mechanic forgets to tighten a screw on some damn-ass airplane in Idaho this weekend and my life is over. I hate airplanes. I won't even look at any. Put Raquel Welch on one wing stark naked and Ursula Andress on the other wing and put the airplane right in front of me, and I wouldn't even look in its direction. I'm like Al's mother—he flies and I worry. Probably I'll die of worrying and he'll fly a loop-de-loop over my grave."

"How did you know each other in school?"

"Oh, he was beautiful. We were roommates as freshmen. He had boxed Golden Gloves. He was very serious. Work, work, work all the time. You'd think he had a little clock wound up inside him, and if he didn't keep time to it, he'd choke or something. I wanted to get into the fraternity and he didn't. I mean, he didn't care. He went home most weekends. To the ribald town, Nonheagan, Pennsylvania. Jesus, what a boring town. I went home with him one weekend. On Saturday night for excitement we went downtown and watched the bus stop. I said, 'Jesus, Al, you're always so serious. College has more to it than just work, work, work.' I wanted to get him to apply to the fraternity with me. I thought I'd have a better chance. They turned me down and made an offer to him. He hadn't even applied. The most crushing blow of my life. I thought I'd never get over it. I mean, how the hell can kids, seventeen, eighteen years old, make decisions like that about someone else after knowing him only a few months? I mean, turning me down? In a few months this bunch of jerks decided Al was all beautiful and good and I was a shit. And Al didn't even spend the weekends on campus. I rushed the fraternity, and the fraternity rushed Al. Jesus, I wept. Al accepted, on condition they accept me too. His roommate. Jesus, I'll never forget that. The sweetest thing anybody ever did for me. But how did he have the balls to do it? It meant so much, and he stood back cool as a cucumber at eighteen and bargained with this bunch of brass monkeys. I thought he'd never carry it off. He did. They accepted us both, they wanted him so bad. Then he never did a damn thing for the fraternity except honor it by living there. He still went home on the weekends. I stayed at the fraternity weekends. Jesus, we had some beautiful times. I'll never forget that."

"I don't understand. What was so great about Alan Stanwyk?"

"What's so great about Alan Stanwyk? He's thirty-three now, and he's running one of the biggest corporations in the world."

"Yeah?"

"Yeah. I know what you're going to say. You're going to say he married Collins Aviation. He's also brilliant, and he's worked like a son of a bitch. I'm proud to live off him."

"Sorry."

90

"Believe me, the Collins family wanted him, needed him more than he needed them. I think if it were a toss-up as to whether he saved Alan or Joan, old John Collins would rescue Alan and send his own daughter to the wolves. Alan would be running Collins Aviation today whether he married Joan Collins or not."

"You really think so?"

"I really do. No question about it. You don't know how able this guy is. Corporations should trip over themselves to get Alan, just like the fraternities did. That guy's got everything."

"You're a hero-worshipper."

"Yes, and Alan Stanwyk is my hero."

"Do you actually see much of him?"

"No, not really. We're interested in different things. He's flying, playing tennis, squash, sailing. I'm interested in drinking. He works hard at his business. But he's still very serious about everything. He's incapable of sitting down and having a casual drink as you and I are doing right now. I mean, we're just talking. You're not trying to learn something; I'm not trying to learn something; we're just shooting the breeze. He has to use every moment for some purpose or other. Also, I don't think Joan is too fond of my wife. I'm not either, of course, the little darling. Jesus. You haven't met my wife. With a little luck, you won't. What can I give you to run away with her?"

"So, Burt, you don't really know an awful lot about what Al's doing or thinking these days."

"I never have. No one ever has. That guy plays awfully close to the chest. He could be dying of cancer and he wouldn't tell you."

"Funny you should say that."

"He wouldn't tell his best friend his pants were on fire."

"I thought Joan was very subdued at lunch."

"Well, let me put it this way: you're a friend of Joan's, and I'm a friend of Al's—right?"

Fletch said, "Right."

"So you see things from her side. I see things from his side."

"Right."

"He didn't just marry the girl of his dreams. He married a corporation. He married a business, an omnipresent father-in-law, a board

91

of directors, a staff of servants, a Racquets Club, Christ knows what else. If the average wife is an anchor, that guy is tied to a whole continent."

"Joan said something about their buying a ranch in Nevada."

"Yes. Al's told me about it. I'm to take over the insurance for it when the deal goes through. Sometime in a couple of weeks. Fifteen million dollars' worth of cows."

"Lucky you."

"All these years I've been worrying about Al's dying. Now I have to worry about cows dying. At least cows don't fly airplanes. Maybe now I should worry about Al's dying of hoof and mouth disease."

"Insuring a Nevada ranch seems a little out of your line."

"Al's been very good to me. I'm supposed to be in touch with the real estate broker out there in a couple of weeks. I forget his name. I've got it written down somewhere inside."

"Jim Swarthout?"

"Yeah. That's the name. You know him?"

"Sure. Nice man."

"Hope he knows more about insuring cows than I do. I need all the help I can get."

"I guess the ranch will give them a chance to get away together. I mean Joan and Alan."

"No. It's just more corporation. It's her idea, you know—the ranch."

"It is?"

"Yeah. Al couldn't care less about it. He knows less about cows than I do, and all I know is that a cow is square with legs sticking out at the corners. He doesn't want the damn place. Rancho Costo Mucho."

"I thought it was his idea."

"Negative."

"Then why is Joan so subdued?"

"What do you mean?"

"Maybe I'm wrong, but I thought she acted sort of sad. Over lunch."

92

"She's worse than he is. Serious, serious, serious. Haven't you ever noticed it before? You'd think with all that money, they'd smile once in a while. It's almost as if they think smiling costs money."

"Sorry I didn't get to meet their daughter, Julie."

"Little brat."

"Little brat?"

"Jesus, I wish she had a sister so I could beat one of them to death with the other one. Have another drink?"

"Burt, no thanks. I've got to go get on that airplane."

"Going back tonight, huh?"

"Just have time to get to the hotel, change, and get to the airport."

"Pity you can't stay and meet my wife. Maybe you'd want to take her with you."

"Nice talking with you, Burt."

"God, she's awful. Don't make it such a long time again, John. Anytime you're in town, drop by."

"I will, Burt. I will."

16

"The fuzz. The fuzz. The fuzz."

Two screwdrivers. A grilled cheese sandwich. Three gin and tonics taken in fast succession. Lying on the beach felt good to Fletch. The sand cooling down in the setting sun had enough warmth to it to permeate his skin, his muscles, his bones. The nearly horizontal rays of the sun were crossed laterally over his body by a twilight breeze.

Unabashedly, he slept.

It was Sando who shook him, saying, "The fuzz. Stash anything you've got. A bust."

Darkness. The bubble lights of the police cars rotated over the sea wall. Silence. Forms carrying riot sticks were ambling down the beach. The people on the beach who were able to move were moving as fast as they could without losing a sense of smoothness, trying not to appear as if they were hurrying away. Some were walking into the ocean. A few went to the edge of the water and strolled one way or the other along it, their profiles on the moonlit surface of the water. The foxes had come into the chicken yard. Fat Sam came to the front of his lean-to and sat cross-legged on the sand. Gummy Montgomery remained propped on his elbows. Fletch did not get up. Nowhere could he see Bobbi's little form.

The police passed to Fletch's right and left. There were seven of them. They wore riot helmets, with the visors pulled down. Chief Cummings, a tall man with heavy shoulders, was with them.

They stood in an imperfect circle around Montgomery. The chief stuck his riot stick into Gummy's stomach and leaned on it, gently.

"Come on, Gummy."

"Jesus Christ. Why me? Why always me?"

"Your Poppa's worried about you."

"Tell him to go fuck off."

"Let's go, Gummy."

The chief leaned harder on his riot stick stuck in Gummy's stomach.

"I don't have anything. Jesus Christ, I'm clean."

The stick was pressed almost to his backbone.

"Harassment!"

Gummy tried to hit the stick away with the side of his forearm but only succeeded in hurting both his forearm and his stomach.

"Harassment. Big word for an eighteen-year-old."

"I'm seventeen. Leave me alone!"

Another policeman, a short, stocky man, suddenly pounced on Gummy, banging his ear with the back of his hand, his fist closed. He began to swing at his head again from the other side.

Gummy scrambled to his feet to escape more blows.

Fletch, having given the matter some thought, went behind the stooping, off-balance policeman and pushed him over. The policeman's head plowed into the sand where Gummy had been lying.

A third policeman, in surprise, turned to swing his riot stick at Fletch.

With full force, Fletch belted the policeman in the stomach.

94

A fourth policeman, a big man, in a gesture of bravado, ripped off his helmet and charged at Fletch bare-fisted. Fletch punched him twice in the face, once in the eye, once on the nose.

Fletch heard a crack. Saw a flash of light. Felt his knees pointing toward the sand. He said, "Shit."

His head was in Bobbi's lap. There were true stars in the sky.

"Jesus," he said.

The beach was quiet.

"Does it hurt?"

He said, "Jesus."

"Sando came and got me. I thought they'd killed you."

"Oh, my God, it hurts."

"He said you belted a policeman."

"Two of them," Fletch said. "Three of them. I'm still on the beach."

"What can I do to help you?" Bobbi asked.

"Shoot me."

"I haven't got any stuff."

Fletch hadn't meant that. He decided to remain misunderstood.

"Why am I still at the beach?"

"You thought you'd be in outer space?"

"I thought I'd be in jail."

"You're all right. They're gone."

"Why didn't they arrest me?"

"I'm glad they didn't."

"I expected them to arrest me. I belted three policemen."

"They would have thrown away the key."

Sando stood over them, his shoulders looking bony in the moonlight. He was eating a hot dog.

"Hey, man. How're ya doin'?"

"What happened?" Fletch asked.

"They arrested Gummy again."

"Did they arrest anyone else?"

"No."

"Why didn't they arrest me?"

"They started to," Sando said. "A couple of the apes began to drag you by your ankles."

"What happened?"

"The chief said to leave you there. I guess dragging you over the sea wall would have been too much work for his precious bastards."

"Christ. They didn't arrest me. How long have they been gone?"

"I don't know. A half hour?"

Bobbi said, "What can I do for you? Should we go back to the pad?"

"You go. I can't move."

"I'll help you," Sando said.

"No. I want to stay here."

"It's Saturday night," Bobbi said. "I should be busy."

She was wearing white shorts, a halter and sandals.

"You go get busy," Fletch said. "I'll be all right."

"Are you sure? I mean, it is Saturday night."

"I'll be all right."

"It's going to be a long night," Sando said. "Fat Sam is fresh out."

Pain, anxiety twinged Bobbi's face. She had built a big need.

"Are you sure?" Fletch said.

"Not even aspirin."

Fletch said, "Christ."

"I'll go work up a couple of tricks anyway." Bobbi's voice shook. "It's Saturday night, and there's always tomorrow."

"Yeah," Sando said. "Sunday."

After Bobbi left, Sando sat silently for a while beside Fletch, saying nothing. Then Sando left.

Fletch built himself a back and head rest in the sand. He was higher on the beach than Fat Sam's lean-to and could see all sides of it. There was a half moon. No one could enter or leave the lean-to without Fletch's seeing him.

The inside of his head felt separated from the outside. Each time he moved or thought of moving his head, the mobile parts hit the stable parts and caused pain.

There was some blood in his hair. Grains of sand had stuck to the blood. During the long night the blood, hair and sand stiffened into a fairly usable abrasive.

After two and a half hours, Fletch gently lifted himself up, walked thirty paces, lowered himself to his knees, and threw up.

Then he walked back to his sand bed.

There was no light in Fat Sam's lean-to.

Someone was walking from the sea wall.

Fletch said, "Creasey."

"Hi." Creasey changed direction slightly and stood over Fletch. "Christ, man. I'm hanging."

Creasey was dressed in blue jean shorts, shirtless, shoeless. He was carrying nothing. Clearly he was carrying nothing.

His hands jerked spasmodically. His eyes moved restlessly. It was true what he had said: he was hanging hellfire.

"Is it true? Fat Sam clean?"

"Yeah."

Creasey said: "I met Bobbi. Jesus Christ."

"You can always try," Fletch said. "Wake the bastard up."

Creasey exhaled deeply. "I've got to. No other way. I've got to see the doctor."

Fletch watched him walk down to the lean-to, bend in the moonlight, walk into the shadow. He heard the voices, one desperate, sharp-edged; the other understanding, conciliatory, cool.

Creasey walked back up to Fletch.

"Jesus," he said. "Nothing. Nothing at all."

"I know."

"Jesus."

Creasey's shoulders were shaking visibly. Shivering.

"Fat Sam said you got fucked by the fuzz. Bobbi said so, too."

"I was cooled."

"Can't you move?"

"Don't want to."

"Fuckin' fuzz."

"They arrested Gummy again."

"Fuckin' fuzz."

Creasey began to take deep breaths. Maybe there was a high to be had in hyperventilation. A relaxation. His stomach went in and his chest filled like a balloon, then collapsed. Again and again. In the moonlight, his eyes were bright.

Fletch said, "Sorry, man."

"You got any?"

"All used."

"Bobbi?"

"You know she has nothing."

"I know she has nothin'. She doesn't store. She uses. Always. Uses."

"What did Fat Sam say?"

"He said he had nothing. Nothing. Nothing."

"When will the candy man come?"

"He said he'd be back in business tomorrow."

"What time tomorrow?"

"Tomorrow morning. Ten. Eleven."

Fletch said, "You'll live."

Creasey said, "Yeah."

He went back up the beach and over the sea wall.

Fletch had had concussions before, and he had suffered shock before, and he had spent nights on the beach before. He dreaded the hours before sunrise. They came. He remained on the beach, overviewing Vatsyayana's lean-to. He forced himself to remain awake. The dew came. His jeans, his shirt became heavily wet. Even the inside of his nose became wet. He was horribly cold. He shivered violently, continuously. Staying awake was then no problem.

He thought of Alan Stanwyk's wanting to die in a few days. His wife, his daughter, his mansion. It was possible, but Fletch had not yet proved it. He had not yet checked everything. Not all the way. He had a good sense of the man, but not yet a complete sense of the man. He tried not to speculate. He went over in his mind, again and again, what he would say into his tape recorder next time. What he knew. What he had checked absolutely. He reviewed all the things he did not know yet, all the facts he had not checked absolutely. There were many such facts. He reviewed his sources. There were not many fresh sources left. He counted the days—four, really, only four—he had left.

Sometime, he would have to sleep. He promised himself sleep. Sometime.

Light came into the sky.

Throughout that night, with the exception of Creasey, who was clearly carrying nothing, no one approached Vatsyayana's lean-to. Fat Sam did not leave the lean-to.

By eight forty-five, Fletch was sweating in the sun.

People drifted onto the beach. Bodies that had remained on the beach all night moved. Some wandered down to the dunes to relieve themselves. Some did not bother to go to the dunes. No one spoke. They looked into each other's eyes and got the message that Fat Sam had not yet received delivery. For a while, Fat Sam sat cross-legged in the opening of his lean-to, taking the morning sun. No one approached him. To a stranger, it would all look like young people sitting silently, half asleep, on the beach on a Sunday morning. Fletch saw the fear, the anxiety, the desperation in the darting eyes; the extraordinary number of cigarettes being smoked; the suppressed shaking of the hands. He heard the shattering silence. Some of these people had been hanging fire two or three days.

At ten-thirty Gummy returned to the beach. He sat alone. Over his long jeans he was wearing a Hawaiian shirt like a tent. His shoulders seemed no wider than the back of his neck. His face in profile was hawkish. He sat absolutely still, staring straight in front of him.

Bobbi came to the beach, and Creasey, and Sando, and July. They sat close to Fletch. No one said a word.

Fat Sam had moved back into the shadow of his lean-to. He had withdrawn.

"Jesus," Sando said.

People began to move toward the lean-to. People in shorts, jeans, shirtless. Bikinis. People carrying nothing but money. The store was open. Fletch had not perceived a signal of any sort. First Creasey. Then Bobbi. They stood around outside the lean-to, not speaking, looking at their feet, their hands, not at each other, ashamed of their desperation. July, Bing Crosby, Gummy, Florida, Filter-tip, Jagger. Fletch stood with them. Milling. In and out of the lean-to. Somebody must have dropped something. There was a supply. Everything. Fat Sam was dealing. People who had been served began to hustle off the beach. Squirrels with nuts to store. They were going to stash. They were going to relieve their tensions. They were going to shoot up.

Fletch backed away, imitating the face of someone who had bought. Who was all right. Bobbi had scurried.

Down the beach, Fletch jumped into the ocean. The morning-cold salt water helped glue the separated parts of his head together. The blood was too congealed to wash out of his hair.

Walking back to his pad, past the Sunday-morning-closed stores of ordinary commerce, he heard the church bells ring. It was Sunday noon and everyone was shooting up.

Fletch slept past midnight.

17

When Fletch woke at a quarter to three Monday morning, he found Bobbi lying in the sleeping bag beside him. He had not heard or felt her come in. It took him a moment to realize she was dead.

The back of his scalp tingling, he scrambled out of the sleeping bag.

As he knelt in the moonlight beside her, his scream choked with horror.

Her eyes appeared to have receded entirely into her head. Her left arm was puffy at the elbow and shoulder. She showed no vital signs.

He guessed she had overdosed.

He spent until dawn ridding the room of every sign of her.

Until eleven o'clock, then, he sat cross-legged on the floor in the center of the room. Rock still. Thinking.

18

Early Monday afternoon, Fletch spent forty minutes under a warm shower in his own apartment. He had driven up from The Beach at about the pace of a hearse. Bobbi was dead and sort of buried. He washed his hair five times. Finally, the blood, the sand, the congealed mess was gone. A crooked, narrow abrasion under his hair was sore to the touch of his fingertips.

Sitting on the divan under the Disderi, he ate two delicatessen sandwiches and drank a bottle of milk. On the coffee table in front of him was the big tape recorder. On the wall across from him was a copy of William James's *Cherry Beach*.

After he had finished his sandwiches and milk, he went into the bedroom and lay on the bed. Facing him was a copy of Fredric Weiss's 1968 photograph of a boy apparently walking in midair beneath two roofs, *Boy Jumping*.

Fletch said, "Bobbi," and picked up the phone and dialed the Nevada number.

"Swarthout Nevada Realty Company."

It was the same voice that had answered Saturday.

"Jim Swarthout, please."

"I'm not sure Mr. Swarthout . . . oh, here he is, sir. One moment, please."

Fletch sat up on the bed. He had to put Bobbi out of mind, now. Lighten his voice. Be convincing.

"Jim Swarthout speaking."

"Hi, Jim. This is Bill Carmichael."

"Bill Carmichael?"

"I'm a stockbroker for a bunch of thieves out here on the Coast known as John Collins and all. The John Collins family."

"Oh, yeah. How are you, Bill?"

"I think we've met," Fletch said.

101

"Well, if you've ever in your life seen an overweight, bald-headed man who was probably drunk at the time, we've met."

"Alan tells me you're doin' a deal with him."

"Alan who?"

"Alan Stanwyk."

"Who's Alan Stanwyk?"

"The guy who married Joan Collins."

"Oh. John's son-in-law."

"Yeah. Anyway, Alan told me about his buying the ranch, and as I might be interested in buying a little piece of real estate out your way myself, I thought I'd give you a ring. The stock market, you know, Jim, isn't all it might be."

"I've never heard from him."

"From whom?"

"Alan what's-his-name. John Collins's son-in-law."

"You've never heard from him?"

"Never. You said he's buying a ranch through me?"

"A big spread. Fifteen million dollars' worth."

"Nope. It's not happening."

"Golly. I thought he said it was quite definite."

"Maybe he's just thinking about it. What's his phone number?"

"Could he be dealing with someone else?"

"No. If there's a fifteen-million-dollar ranch for sale anywhere in Nevada, I'd know about it. There isn't one."

"Amazing."

"I'd know if such a property were available anywhere in the state. And right now there just isn't one. Let me say that over. I can almost perfectly guarantee you that nowhere in the state of Nevada at the present time is there a piece of real estate of such value being sold or bought. Of course there is always the chance of a private deal, between friends or family, where a broker isn't being used or consulted. But even then, I would be very much surprised if I hadn't heard about it."

"In any case, Alan Stanwyk is definitely not using you or your office to buy any real estate in Nevada?"

"Definitely not. As I say, we've never heard from him. I'm sure we could find something for him, though."

"Do me a favor, Jim?"

"Sure."

"Don't call him. You'd just be embarrassing me, and him, too. He mentioned it by the pool last night. He'd had a drink."

"Talking big, huh?"

"I suspect so."

"That's the way it is with these professional in-laws. Always talking about what they're going to do with somebody else's money."

"I guess so. He'd had a drink."

"Well, if he ever gets serious, and if he ever gets his hands on any of his father-in-law's money, send him out to me."

"I will, Jim."

"Now, Bill, you said you were interested in a piece of property yourself."

"I don't know what to say, Jim."

"You were just checking on the old boy."

"Something like that, Jim."

"What are you, the family financial nursemaid?"

"Let's just say I asked a question."

"And you got an answer. I understand. My own daughter is taking art lessons in Dallas, Texas, for Christ's sake."

"Families, Jim. Families."

"I wouldn't trade jobs with you, Bill. But call anytime you want. If old John's hired you to nursemaid Alan what's-his-name, it's all right with me. Just wish I could hire you myself."

"You're a sharp man, Jim. I owe you a drink."

"John Collins does. And from him, I'll accept."

Fletch returned to the living room and sat heavily on the divan. He continued to have a mild headache.

Snapping on the microphone in his hand, he leaned back and closed his eyes. He spoke slowly.

"Although it is my instinct at this point to ramble on regarding the nature of truth, particularly the illusory nature of truth, I shall do my best to confine the following remarks concerning the Alan Stanwyk Murder Mystery to facts as I now know them.

"One comment only for file, which may concern the nature of

103

truth in general, or may, more significantly, concern the nature of facts specifically concerning Alan Stanwyk, to wit: almost every fact adequately confirmed about Alan Stanwyk has also been adequately denied.

"In the case of almost each fact, it would have been easy to accept simple confirmation from an authoritative source. Further checking, however, frequently has resulted in an equally authoritative denial of that fact.

"By now, in my investigation of Alan Stanwyk, I have talked, either in person or by telephone, with his secretary, his personal physician, his father, his wife, his father-in-law, his insurance man who is also his old college roommate. Indirectly, through a third party, I have had testimony from the man's stockbroker. I have had corporate and personal financial views of Stanwyk, and a social view of himself and his wife. I have had a police report on him.

"To the best of my ability, I have run this investigation-in-depth on him without there being any way of his knowing he's being investigated. I have used different names, different identities, and never have I pressed the questioning far enough for the person being questioned to be suspicious, with the exception of Jim Swarthout in Nevada, and I believe I completely cooled his suspicions. He will not report the inquiry to either Stanwyk or his family.

"The portrait of Alan Stanwyk that has emerged so far is that of a bright, healthy, energetic, ambitious man. A man solid in his community, family and business. I would even say a decent man. In fact, perhaps going a bit further than I should, a man of deep loyalties and principles.

"First, he has a clean police record, with the exceptions of a six-month-old unpaid parking ticket from the City of Los Angeles and the complaint that as a lieutenant in the Air Force he buzzed a house with a training jet in San Antonio, Texas.

"From his stockbroker, William Carmichael, we know that Alan Stanwyk is in pretty good financial condition. On paper, he may presently be worth as much as a million dollars. Eventually, because of both the nature of his employment and the nature of his marriage, he will both achieve personal wealth and share in, probably control, one of the world's great fortunes. Even with this ultimate circumstance inevitable, and despite maintaining the highest standard of living available for his immediate family, Stanwyk has salted away over one hundred thousand dollars from salary over a very few years. The last few years, he must have been putting away twenty or twenty-five thousand dollars a year, simply because he hasn't needed it.

"This indicates, at least to me, that such a vice as compulsive gambling can be ruled out. The crime of embezzlement does not seem necessary. Apparently, Stanwyk is not being blackmailed.

"We have from his family physician, and others, good evidence that Stanwyk does not have a drinking problem or a drug problem. Not only is he under consistent close scrutiny by professionals and others who depend upon Stanwyk's physical and mental performance; his way of life, his known, witnessed habits preclude his harboring such addictions. No one can play squash and tennis, sail, and especially fly experimental aircraft with reflexes and nerves shot by depressants.

"I think I can state as a fact that Alan Stanwyk drinks and smokes moderately. Period.

"For what it is worth, from what must be called a streetwalker in the town in which he is currently living, The Hills, a young girl named Roberta 'Bobbi' Sanders had never seen Alan Stanwyk. It might therefore be said that he is not known to have frequented, or cruised, the sexual meat market most convenient to his residence.

"This does not mean that Alan Stanwyk's sexual activity is confined to the marital bed. There is good reason to suspect otherwise.

"However, it does indicate that Alan Stanwyk's sexual activities are controlled in acceptable social patterns.

"His stockbroker and presumed confidant, William Carmichael, doubts strongly that Alan Stanwyk maintains an extramarital sex life. Carmichael believes such an extramarital sex life would place in jeopardy Stanwyk's relations with his wife and thus with his father-in-law employer.

"However, without meaning to visit the sins of the wife upon the husband, I had the distinct impression that his wife, Joan Stanwyk, was perfectly willing to enjoy a sexual dalliance with this investigator. Her ardor may have been the result of tennis followed by martinis. This should be more thoroughly checked later. One expects that if a wife is playing around, a husband is, although the reverse is not always true. If the wife is playing around as openly as it seems, at least she would have little to complain about the husband's extramarital affairs.

"We also have testimony from a contemporary of Stanwyk's father-in-law, *News-Tribune* society writer Amelia Shurcliffe, that extramarital affairs on the part of either Alan or Joan Stanwyk would not greatly disturb John Collins. Apparently the old boy has every reason of his own to be most understanding regarding such matters. According to Mrs. Shurcliffe, his own sexual activities have not been entirely confined to the marital bed.

"Other matters concerning Alan Stanwyk's health are more confusing.

"So far, the only evidence that Alan Stanwyk has terminal cancer is from Alan Stanwyk's own mouth.

"His personal physician denies it. I take that back: his personal physician, Dr. Joseph Devlin of the Medical Center, states that as far as he knows, Alan Stanwyk is in perfect health. He states he has not referred him to any specialist—ever. He also states he has not given him a complete physical examination recently enough to be viable.

"His insurance company examines him every six months.

"Stanwyk's insurance agent and old college chum, Burt Eberhart, also states that Alan Stanwyk is in perfect physical condition. Although he did make an interesting slip, Freudian or otherwise. He said, 'Al plays so close to the chest, he wouldn't tell you if he were dying of cancer . . .'

"I have since confirmed that Dr. Joseph Devlin is heavily invested in Collins Aviation. My source is Joan Collins Stanwyk. I have confirmed from several sources that if it were known that Stanwyk is terminally ill, at least until Stanwyk has a chance to prepare the company for his absence, Collins Aviation would be in financial trouble.

"Burt Eberhart, besides being Stanwyk's personal insurance man, is the broker for all Collins Aviation insurance. One can presume Eberhart is also heavily invested in Collins Aviation.

"Mentioning cancer casually to Stanwyk's wife, father, and father-in-law caused no discernible reaction. Unless everyone is a very good actor, and superbly in control of his emotions, or in complete ignorance, the people closest to Alan Stanwyk are not thinking of cancer in relation to him.

"Therefore, this investigation is drawing a complete blank.

"No aberrations or abnormalities are apparent thus far in Alan Stanwyk's financial, sexual or health areas.

"Alan Stanwyk's social relations seem splendid. According to society writer Amelia Shurcliffe, the Stanwyks present a rather nice, solid, possibly dull image. She even believes they may be in love with each other. Alan Stanwyk could not have fitted into this society of extreme wealth and responsibility without undergoing intensive envious scrutiny. He must have a good glovemaker. Clearly, he has not committed the faux pas of ostentation, silliness, aloofness, what-have-you. He is generally admired and respected.

"The same is true among his intimates. I would say he is intensely admired among family and close friends. Not that he is without criticism. His wife wishes he had more time for her. His father-in-law wishes he had a better sense of humor. His father wishes he wouldn't spend so much time on the telephone. His old friend Burt Eberhart wishes Alan weren't always so serious. Everyone wishes he would stop flying experimental aircraft.

"More publicly, the fact that he married the boss's daughter does not go unnoticed. But as someone pointed out: someone had to. And, after listening to Burt Eberhart, Carradine, Carmichael and John Collins himself, I would guess Alan Stanwyk is the best thing that has ever happened to Collins Aviation. The score seems balanced.

"Alan Stanwyk is not taking a free ride, as one such as Jim Swarthout of Swarthout Nevada Realty is quick to assume.

"Now for a few of the contradictions in facts this investigation thus far has revealed.

"Alan Stanwyk says he is dying of terminal cancer. No one else says so. If he is, no one else knows it.

"Stanwyk's wife and father-in-law say that Stanwyk is estranged from his parents. Yet he visits them all the way across the country every six weeks.

"The reason given for the estrangement is that his father forced him to box. Yet his father insists he urged Alan not to box.

"Despite the fact, confirmed by a call to the Nonheagan Inn, that Alan visits his parents every six weeks, he has never told them that he has a child and that they have a grandchild.

"Everyone says that Alan Stanwyk is buying a ranch in Nevada—his wife, his father-in-law, his stockbroker, his insurance man. Everyone, that is, except the person whom both Stanwyk's wife and insurance man identify as the real estate broker: Jim Swarthout. It was quite clear from his attitude, as well as from his explicit statements, that Swarthout has never done business with, or even met, Alan Stanwyk.

"To some extent, these contradictions can be explained, now that we have some knowledge of the man.

"I take the clue from Burt Eberhart's statement: 'Al plays so close to his chest he wouldn't tell you he was dying of cancer.'

"Although no one knows it, Alan Stanwyk could have terminal cancer.

"There can be an answer to his strange relations with his parents. He could love them very much. Being an only son, he could have a profound sense of loyalty and duty toward them. Apparently he has for his old college roommate, Burt Eberhart. As Marvin Stanwyk says, he could find stopping off in his old hometown frequently a restful experience.

"At the same time, he could realize that the world of Joan and John Collins is no place for Marvin and what's-her-name Mother Stanwyk. He might feel they would be very out-of-place and very embarrassed. Therefore, he might have fudged the date of his wedding, not told them they were grandparents, and told everyone else he was estranged from his parents—solely to save their feelings.

"There is even an answer to the mysterious ranch in Nevada. He could have started to buy the ranch in Nevada for the best reason in the world: a good real estate investment. Neither he nor Joan needed to like the idea of living on a ranch. Thus the confusion in everybody's mind about whose idea the ranch is—Alan's or Joan's. Neither of them really wants to do it. Buying the ranch is simply a good business idea.

108

"It is possible he took the first steps toward buying the ranch, which first steps for him would have been seeking the advice of his stockbroker, insurance man, wife and father-in-law. After he did this much, he discovered he was dying of cancer. He had to devote his time and energies to cleaning shop at Collins Aviation, subtly, so that no one knew what he was doing. That would take some effort. He knew he would not be able to see the land purchase through, but he could not tell people so without also telling them why, that he has terminal cancer. Therefore, he kept talking about it as if it were a real, developing thing. John Collins referred him to Jim Swarthout. It is very likely that subsequently, when John Collins or whoever asked about Swarthout and the ranch, Stanwyk answered, 'Yes, yes, everything's fine.' Doubtless he even found himself agreeing to take his wife to the ranch next weekend when there isn't any ranch, because Stanwyk knows that for him there isn't any next weekend.

"Even the contradictions can be made to go together.

"Yet there remains one overwhelming question in my mind.

"If Alan Stanwyk wishes to commit suicide, why doesn't he die the way everybody half-expects him to die?

"Why doesn't he crash an airplane?"

Still moving slowly, Fletch disposed of his sandwich wrappings and carton of milk.

In the bedroom, he carefully packed a large suitcase. Into it went tennis whites. Three pairs of blue jeans. Blue jean shorts. T-shirts. Several dress shirts. Neckties. Underwear. His shaving kit. Two suits. Two sports jackets. Two pairs of slacks. His address book. Black shoes. Three pairs of black socks. Three pairs of brown socks. His passport.

He put typing paper and carbon paper into his typewriter case and closed it.

Then he dressed in brown loafers, brown socks, a dress shirt, necktie, trousers and a sports jacket. And sunglasses.

Taking his big tape recorder, typewriter case and suitcase, he went to the apartment garage. He lashed the tape recorder to the passenger seat of the MG. He put the typewriter case behind the front seats and the suitcase in the trunk.

Then he drove to the main gate of Collins Aviation and waited.

19

It was four o'clock when Fletch pulled up and parked across from the main gate of Collins Aviation.

At four forty-five, through sunglasses, he saw the gray-uniformed guard at the gate step briskly out of his guardhouse, whistle and wave people aside, clear the road and the sidewalk, and casually salute a car coming through. It was the gray Jaguar XKE, license number 440-001. It turned left into traffic.

Alan Stanwyk was driving.

Fletch followed him.

Joan Stanwyk had said Alan worked late Mondays and Wednesdays. On those two days of the week he seldom arrived home before midnight. He remained at the office.

It was Monday. Stanwyk had left the office before five.

He continued down Stevenson to Main and turned right on Main. Following him, Fletch thought Stanwyk might be heading for the expressway toward the city. But after twelve blocks, Stanwyk turned left on Seabury. At the corner of Seabury and Bouvard he pulled into the parking lot of a liquor store. Fletch waited across the street.

Watching Stanwyk amble into the liquor store and out again, Fletch could only think him a well man. An unconcerned man. A relaxed man. As he went in, Stanwyk's hands were in the pockets of his slacks. His gait was slow and even. His face expressionless. When he came out, his face had the half smile of someone who had just passed pleasantries. In the bag he was carrying were at least three bottles of liquor. It took him a moment to find the right key on his keychain for the ignition.

Continuing the way he had been going, Stanwyk went another three blocks on Seabury and then turned left on Putnam. A half mile along Putnam, he turned into the tree-shaded parking lot of a garden apartment development. He parked the Jaguar in the shade of the trees at the far side of the parking lot. Fletch parked in the middle row of the parking lot, in the sunlight. Stanwyk locked his car.

Carrying the bag of liquor, he strolled across the parking lot, cutting through the middle row of cars within three cars of Fletch, walked fifteen yards down the sidewalk, turned left on a walk and into a doorway.

Fletch waited ten minutes by his dashboard clock.

Then he went into the doorway himself.

The doorway served two apartments. On the left, the name on the letterbox was Charles Rice. The box was full of mail.

The mailbox on the right was empty. The name on that box was Sandra Faulkner.

A sign in the recessed doorway warned trespassers and solicitors as well as loiterers and burglars. It was signed GREENE BROS. MANAGEMENT.

"Where's Gummy?"

Someone had gotten up enough energy to make a campfire on the beach. It was a reasonably cool night. Farther up the beach there were other campfires.

Vatsyayana said, "Fletch."

In a corner of the parking garage, Fletch had changed into jeans. Having had a sport coat on, he had not realized it had gotten cooler. He wished he had at least put on a T-shirt.

"Where's Gummy?" he asked again.

July said, "I saw him earlier."

"Where did he go? Did he say?"

July said, "No."

"Anyone else seen Gummy?"

No one answered.

Vatsyayana asked, "Where's Bobbi?"

Fletch said, "She's split."

"For where?"

Vatsyayana's look was one of kindly concern.

"That great candy store in the sky."

Vatsyayana said nothing.

Rolled against the base on the sea wall in a blanket, not far from where Fletch had placed the rock the night before, was Creasey.

Fletch stood over him a moment in the dark, not sure whether Creasey was traveling or asleep.

Creasey said, "What's happening, man?"

"I'm looking for Gummy," Fletch said.

"Oh, man, he's gone."

"What do you mean, gone?"

"That kid's had it. I mean, how often can you be a beatin' bag for the fuzz?"

"You don't know he's gone."

Creasey said, "He should have gone. Man, there has to be enough of everything. I mean, the kid's been beatin' and been beatin'. Then he gets home and his daddy whumps him. Everybody's beatin' up on that kid all the time."

Fletch said, "I'm lookin' for Gummy."

"Like my old skins. Man, I feel guilty for beatin' on them. Every night with sticks. Drumsticks. I beat on those skins. I mean, how do we know those skins don't have feeling? Suppose when I hit them they hurt? Really hurt?"

"I don't know about that, Creasey."

"I've got a lot of painin' to do. To make up for what I did."

"Don't you think the drums will forgive you?"

"The Christly drums. That's the idea. Beat up on anybody, anything, as much as you want, even drums, and they must forgive you, because that's what The Man said. Christ."

"I'm looking for Gummy. Have you seen him?"

"No. Where's Bobbi?"

Fletch said, "She's all right."

"She split? I haven't seen her in weeks."

"You saw her yesterday morning."

"Yeah. She was all strung out. She'd had it. Fletch? You know, she'd had it. Last time I saw her."

"I didn't realize it."

"She'd had it. Is she gone?"

"Yeah. She's gone."

"Jesus."

Fletch stood a moment in the dark near Creasey, not looking at the rock, and then moved on.

At another campfire he sat down and waited a moment before speaking. No one was speaking.

"Anyone seen Gummy?"

No one answered.

The kid with the jug ears they called Bing Crosby was looking expectantly at Fletch, as if waiting to hear what Fletch had just said.

"I'm looking for Gummy."

A forty-year-old man with a telephone receiver stenciled on his sweater, with the words under it DIAL ME, said, "He's not here."

Fletch waited a moment before moving on.

At another campfire, Filter-tip said he thought Gummy had gone home. To his parents' house. Jagger said he thought Gummy had been picked up by the police again.

When Fletch stood up from the campfire, he found Vatsyayana standing behind. Vatsyayana walked a few paces with him toward the sea wall.

"Why are you looking for Gummy?"

"Bobbi gave me a message for him."

"Where's Bobbi?"

"She's split."

"Where's Bobbi?"

"Gonzo. Bye-bye."

"Where?"

"With a knapsack I gave her. Full of protein tablets and Ritz crackers I ripped off from a Seventh Day Adventist supermarket."

Vatsyayana stopped. "I said, where's Bobbi?"

"Look. She got her supply up yesterday, didn't she?"

"Yeah."

"So she split."

Vatsyayana was giving him the hard stare through the moonlight. His eyes remained kind.

"Why are you looking for Gummy?"

"I told you. Bobbi gave me a message for him."

"What's the message?"

"It's for Gummy."

"Tell me."

Fletch said, "Hang loose, Fat Sam."

He followed his moon shadow up the beach.

On that cool night, trying to sleep on his groundmat, Fletch missed his sleeping bag. He missed Bobbi. Together they would have been warm in the sleeping bag.

20

Fletch heard the heavy footsteps on the stairs. They were in no hurry. They came along the short landing to his door and stopped.

The door swung open slowly.

Two policemen looked through the door.

Fletch sat up.

"Good morning," the first policeman said. They both looked showered, shaved and full of coffee.

"What day is it?" Fletch asked.

"Tuesday."

The second policeman was looking for a place to sit down. In his eyes going over the room was comparable pride in his own home, his own furniture.

"Get ready to come with us."

"Why?"

"The chief wants to see you. Questioning."

Fletch was looking at his bare feet on their sides on the groundmat.

"I guess I'm ready."

"You don't even want to take a leak?"

Fletch said, "Why should I take a leak when I'm going to the police station anyway?"

It was about a quarter to seven in the morning.

One of the policemen held open the back door of the patrol car for Fletch and closed it after he had gotten in.

A heavy wire grill ran between the front seat and the back seat.

The back seat was broken down. It smelled of vomit. Dried blood was on the seat and the floor.

Fletch said, "This is a very poor environment back here. I want you to know that."

"It's nice up here," said the policeman in the passenger seat.

The driver said, "How's your head?"

Fletch had forgotten.

"This is the first time it hasn't hurt. You two aren't the two I belted on the beach the other night, are you?"

"No," said the driver. "I'm the one who belted you."

Fletch said, "You do nice work."

"It's a pleasure."

"How come you guys didn't arrest me the other night?"

"The chief said not to," said the driver. "He was feeling mellow."

"He feels mellow every time he comes back from his retirement home in Mexico. He counts the grapefruit or something. Makes him feel mellow."

"He's retiring soon?"

"Next year sometime."

Fletch said, "I was hoping he'd retire before I got to the station."

They turned onto Main. It was difficult talking through a grill to the backs of heads. Fletch wanted to open the window, but the window jack handles had been removed. The police were probably afraid someone would try to commit suicide by bopping himself on the nose with one.

The smell was beginning to make Fletch feel sick.

He repeated, "This is a very poor environment back here."

From his appearance, Chief of Police Graham Cummings could not have been anything else. Short-cropped iron-gray hair. A jawline like a shovel scoop. Broad, massive shoulders. Steady, brown eyes. A man of his appearance in any town would almost automatically be given the job of police chief.

"What's your name?"

"Fletch."

"What's your full name?"

"Fletch Fletch Fletch."

Alone in the chief's bare, utilitarian office, they sat on either side of a gray aluminum desk.

"By any chance, could Fletch be short for Fletcher?"

"It could be."

"Is Fletcher your first name or your last?"

"My first name."

"What's your last name?"

"Smith."

"Fletcher Smith," the Chief said. "Seems I've heard that name somewhere before."

"Fletcher Smith?"

"No. Just Smith. Where do you live, Smith?"

"I forget the address. Where your goons picked me up this morning."

"You live there?"

"Weekends I spend in Hawaii."

"Do you live alone?"

"Except for a pet roach."

"And what do you do for a living, Mr. Smith?"

"I'm a shoeshine boy."

"There was no shoeshine equipment in your room."

"I must have been ripped off during the night. I'll file a complaint before I leave."

The chief said, "There seems to be a certain lack of coordination between yourself and your office, Mr. Fletcher."

"I beg your pardon?"

"Your superiors at the *News-Tribune* called here yesterday. Your editor. A Mrs. Snow. Do I have that right? A Clara Snow."

"Shit."

"She informed me you are doing an investigation, for your newspaper, of drugs on the beach. And she asked that we keep an eye out for you. She said she thought you might be getting close to something. If you asked for police protection we were to understand who you are, and to give it."

"Shit."

"You are I.M. Fletcher of the *News-Tribune.*"

"You've got the wrong I.M. Fletcher."

"Are you getting close to something, Mr. Fletcher?"

"No."

"Well, Mr. Fletcher."

"Fuck."

The chief did not relax. He remained, forearms on the desk, looking directly at Fletch.

"Mr. Fletcher, it seems you have forgotten certain things. There is a certain little rule, shall we call it, which says that you are supposed to identify yourself as a journalist immediately to any officer of the law with whom you find yourself in conversation—even casual conversation. Had you forgotten that rule?"

"It slipped my mind."

"We have you on a violation of that rule, Mr. Smith."

"Entrapment."

"Second, we know that you have been living here at The Beach with a young girl named Bobbi."

"I have?"

"Where is Bobbi?"

"She split."

"Where did Bobbi go?"

"I don't know. Home, maybe."

"I sincerely doubt that. Addicts seldom stray far from their source."

"She got a bit ahead. Enough to trip on."

"When did she leave?"

"Sunday night."

"By what method of transportation?"

"She flew."

"Then there is the fact that we found stashed in your room quantities of both marijuana and heroin."

"Did you have a search warrant?"

"We weren't searching. We just happened to find the stuff concealed in the stove."

"I was hiding it from Bobbi."

117

"You are guilty of possession of hard drugs."

"I made the purchases as evidence."

"From whom did you buy it?"

"Fat Sam."

"Then why was the marijuana in City Police Laboratory bags?"

"Who knows Fat Sam's source?"

"Why would you need to make a purchase of marijuana anyway? One purchase of heroin would be sufficient evidence."

"I like to write a balanced story."

"That story you wrote last fall about the Police Association wasn't very balanced."

"What?"

"I remember the story. And the by-line. I. M. Fletcher. You said the Police Association was nothing but a drinking club."

"Oh."

"You made very little of the fact that we have seminars, when we meet, on police techniques. That we raise money for the Police Academy. That last year we donated an ambulance to Ornego, California."

"Thanks for reading me."

"Do you get my point, Mr. Fletcher?"

"I'm getting it."

"I want you out of town. Immediately."

"Some police protection."

"You may have some excuses for the matters I have already mentioned, including the possession of heroin, but I have on my staff three police officers who can attest to having been struck by you while in the course of their duty last Sunday night."

"You didn't arrest me then."

"We were trying to subdue another prisoner."

"It took seven of you to subdue a seventeen-year-old junkie?"

"Due to your intercession, three of the seven were wounded."

"Why didn't you arrest me the other night?"

"Did you want to be arrested, Mr. Fletcher?"

"Golly, gee, no, chief."

"Mr. Fletcher, I am going to give you two orders, and you are going to obey both. The first is that any evidence you have regarding drugs on the beach you turn over to us. Do you have any evidence at all?"

"No."

"None?"

"Just Fat Sam."

"You really aren't very good at your work, are you?"

"I get a lot of help from the office."

"The second order is that you get out of town before noon. And not come back. Ever. Is that clear?"

"What are you afraid of?"

"We're not afraid of you."

"Seems like it."

"We are conducting our own investigation of the drugs on the beach, Mr. Fletcher. This is police work. These investigations have been ongoing for some time."

"Two or three years."

"We're looking for a break sometime in the next few months. This is a difficult, complicated business. A private investigation, even by your newspaper, could ruin all our work to date. I think I've made myself clear: get out of town, or we'll run you through a course that will begin immediately with jail, and will end with your suffering a very long and very expensive legal battle. Possession of heroin and assault upon three separate officers while in performance of their duties should be enough to convince you."

"I'm convinced."

"You will leave town immediately?"

"Never to darken your dungeon again."

21

It was a quarter to nine, and the sidewalks were as full as they ever got in the business district of The Beach. Traffic on Main Street was bumper to bumper.

119

A block and a half from the police station, an approaching gray Jaguar XKE slid against the curb. License number 440-001. The car Fletch was to steal after murdering Alan Stanwyk in sixty hours. The horn honked.

Fletch got into the front seat.

Stanwyk moved the car back into the line of traffic.

"What were you doing at the police station?"

"Being questioned."

"About what?"

"A kid I know disappeared. A girl named Bobbi."

"Are you involved in her disappearance?"

"No, but I sure want to get out of town soon. How did you know I was at the police station?"

"I asked at the beer stand. Which was open at eight o'clock in the morning. Some life you lead. A kid with jug ears said he saw you this morning in the back of a patrol car."

"French fries are good for breakfast."

Again Stanwyk lit a cigarette without using the dashboard lighter. He used a gold lighter from his pocket. He was wearing sunglasses.

Fletch said, "What do you want?"

"To see how everything's going. Do you have your passport?"

"I should have it tomorrow."

"And the gloves?"

"I'll get a pair."

"You *have* applied for the passport?"

"Oh, yes, I even had my picture taken."

"Fine. Are you clear in your mind about what you are going to do?"

"Perfectly. You still want it done?"

Stanwyk blew out a stream of smoke. "Yes."

"Are you sure you're dying of cancer?"

"Yes. Why do you ask?"

"You look fine."

"It takes a while for it to show. I want to be gone by then."

They were sitting at a red light.

"I remember reading that you fly airplanes," Fletch said. "Test airplanes. Whatever you call them."

"What about it?"

The car crossed the intersection.

"So why don't you kill yourself in an airplane?"

The shoulders of Stanwyk's suit jacket moved more than another man's would when he shrugged. He had powerful shoulders.

"Call it pride, if you like. If you spend your life trying to keep airplanes in the air, it's sort of difficult to aim one for the ground."

"An expensive pride."

"People have spent more than fifty thousand dollars on pride before."

"I guess so."

"You remember where the house is?"

"At the end of Berman Street."

"That's right. And how are you going to get there?"

"I'm going to take a taxi to the corner of Hawthorne and Main and walk from there. It's a different district, but only about two miles away."

"Good for you. And you remember the flight number?"

"No. You never gave it to me."

Stanwyk was looking at him through the sunglasses. "It's the eleven o'clock TWA flight to Buenos Aires."

"I know that," Fletch said. "But I don't know the number."

Stanwyk said, "Neither do I."

He glided the car against the curb.

"I don't believe you and I should know each other too well," he said. "I'm trying not to know you. What I mean is, I think you should forget what you read about me in the newspapers."

Fletch said, "I just happened to remember that."

"Forget it. I'll let you off here."

"We're on the other side of town. I was going in the other direction."

"You can hitchhike back."

"Thanks a lot."

Stanwyk said, "See you Thursday night."

22

Fletch rang the bell of 15641B Putnam Street and looked back the few feet to where his MG was parked at the curb. Through sunglasses, the green of the car seemed the same as the green of the lawn.

An elfin voice said, "Yes? Who is it?"

Fletch bent and shouted into the mouthpiece: "Greene Brothers Management, Miss Faulkner."

"Just a minute."

Fletch smoothed his tie beneath his buttoned suit jacket.

Sandra Faulkner's face was not particularly friendly when she opened the door. She was wearing black slacks and a loose blouse. Her hair was bleached blond and touseled.

Fletch was astonished. Sandra Faulkner was nowhere near as attractive as Joan Collins Stanwyk. She must be better in bed.

"I'm from Greene Brothers Management," he said sternly.

She said nothing. She was looking at him as if he were a piece of month-old fish.

"The people who manage these apartments."

"So what do you want?"

"We want to talk with you."

"Do you have some identification?"

"If I were you, miss, I would not take this opportunity to be insolent."

"What?"

"We've had complaints from the neighbors about you, and we're here to discuss the possibility of evicting you on morals charges."

"You must be kidding."

"We are not kidding at all. Now, if you wish to continue standing here on the doorstep talking about it, it's all right with me. If you prefer to go inside, out of earshot of your neighbors, we can."

She drew back, leaving the door open.

He entered and closed the door.

"What in God's name are you talking about?"

"You know perfectly well what I'm talking about," he said. "Are you alone now?"

"Jesus Christ!"

He stalked into the living room, which was furnished in what once had been termed Danish modern.

"The use of foul and abusive language will do nothing to further your defense."

"Defense? What defense?"

He pushed open the door of the bathroom, which struck him as peculiarly empty. In the bedroom was a king-size bed, with a mirror suspended from the ceiling over it. The bed was made, at ten-thirty, with a red silk coverlet smoothed over it. On a sideboard in the kitchen was a used bottle of vermouth, a half-empty bottle of vodka, and an empty bottle of California chablis.

"What in Christ's name are you talking about?" Sandra Faulkner asked.

"What's that suspended from the ceiling of the bedroom?"

"It's a mirror. What-the-hell business is it of yours what it is?"

"Miss Faulkner, your lease precisely prohibits hanging anything from the ceiling of this apartment."

"Jesus."

Nowhere in the apartment were there signs of anyone packing.

Fletch sat on a living room chair. He took a notebook and pen out of his pocket.

"Is your real name Sandra Faulkner?"

"Yes. Of course. What's all this about, anyway?"

"Miss Faulkner, you live in a residential community. There are young families who live in these apartments around you. Families with young children."

"I know. So what?"

"It has become clear to some of the mothers, and, I might add, some of the fathers, that you have no visible means of support."

"Jesus."

"You haven't worked in some time."

"Why is that anybody's business?"

"There is a question of whether your hanging around all the time is good for the moral fiber of the community's young."

"Wow. Who'd believe this?"

"Second, it is quite clear what your means of support are. You keep this apartment solely by your means to sexually entertain."

"My God! You're something from the last century."

"Greene Brothers Management is responsible for these apartments, Miss Faulkner, and responsible to some extent for what goes on inside them. At least we must be responsive to complaints."

"You can just get the hell out of here."

Fletch said, "How long have you known Alan Stanwyk?"

Her face changed from fury to suppressed horror mingled with sickness.

"Sit down, Miss Faulkner."

She did. On the edge of the divan.

"How do you know about Alan?"

"Neighbors recognized him. His picture is frequently in the newspapers, after all."

"Jesus. Leave Alan out of this."

"He is paying for this apartment and your support, isn't he?"

"Yes."

"All right, then. You're keeping this apartment through illicit means. You had better tell us everything."

"Why?"

"Miss Faulkner, would you like to see Alan Stanwyk named in an eviction action? An eviction action taken on moral grounds?"

"Oh, my God. I can't believe this is happening. Who complained?"

"It is our policy not to report that sort of thing."

"Make the world safe for informers, huh?"

"We're very grateful to people who tell us when things are amiss among our apartments. How else would we know? Now, I suggest that you take our attempt to grant you a fair hearing sincerely, and tell us all."

124

Sandra Faulkner was looking at Fletch as a lady-in-waiting caught rolling in the hay with a court violinist might have looked at Queen Victoria.

"Do you always wear your sunglasses in the house?" she asked.

"I have a failing in the eyes," Fletch said, "which is not a subject for general conversation."

"I see. Wow. Okay. What do you want to know? I used to work as a receptionist at Collins Aviation. Alan Stanwyk is sort of important at Collins Aviation."

"We know, Miss Faulkner."

"I'm not Miss Faulkner. I'm Mrs. Faulkner. My husband was a test pilot. For the navy. One day, trying to land on an aircraft carrier, he missed and crashed. I couldn't work for a long time thereafter. Jack and I had put off having children, thinking there would be plenty of time . . ."

"This person you refer to as Jack was your husband?"

"My husband. The insurance ran out. Unemployment ran out. I was drinking heavily. Very heavily. At first, Alan Stanwyk's office would make a call to see how I was doing. It was just professional courtesy, I think. One morning, very early, I was drunk out of my mind, and I told the secretary to go fuck herself. The next day, Alan Stanwyk showed up at the door with his secretary and some flowers. This was more than a year after Jack had died. They put me in a hospital for a while. And paid for it. Alan is a flier himself. He was overseas. He has a scar on his belly from where he was wounded. The day I was released, Alan picked me up in his car and brought me home. It's been that way ever since."

"You see him twice a week?"

"Yes, about that. He's given me something to live for. Himself. I hope someday to have his child."

"He comes here on Mondays and Wednesdays?"

"The neighbors don't miss much, do they? The sons of bitches."

"Mrs. Faulkner, do you have any intention of ever marrying Mr. Stanwyk?"

"Why, no. He's married. Joan Collins. He couldn't divorce her. She's the daughter of the chairman of the board, or something. John Collins."

"You've never thought of marrying him?"

"No. We've never discussed it."

"Yet you hope to have his child?"

"Yes. There's nothing wrong with that."

"Are you currently pregnant?"

"No."

"In other words, Mrs. Faulkner, you intend to maintain this affair, unchanged, in this apartment, for the foreseeable future?"

"Yes. I do."

"And Mr. Stanwyk has not indicated to you any desire for change?"

"What do you mean?"

"Well, it hardly needs pointing out, Mrs. Faulkner, you have no rights here. Alan Stanwyk could disappear next week, and you wouldn't have a leg to stand on."

"Fine. If that's what he wants to do. He owes me nothing. I could get a job now. I'm fine."

"Is Mr. Stanwyk in good health?"

"Yes. Terrific. I wish I hadn't let myself go so long."

"And has he indicated any change in your relationship in the foreseeable future?"

"What do you mean?"

"Has he indicated to you that you might be taking a trip together?"

"No. I think I'm kept pretty much in the background. And I've never asked for any such thing."

Fletch closed his notebook. He had written nothing in it.

"Very well, Mrs. Faulkner. I'll make my report to Greene Brothers. I will ask them not to take any action on this matter, as it seems to be a discreet, adult affair."

"Thank you."

"There aren't any other men who use this facility, are there?"

"By 'this facility,' do you mean this apartment, or me? The answer is no to both."

126

"I see." Fletch stood up. "Thank you very much, Mrs. Faulkner."

She said, "You have a lousy management company."

"What did you say?"

"I said you have a lousy management company. Not only are you nosy parkers, but these apartments are not adequately protected against burglary."

"Why do you say that?"

"I was robbed last night."

"You were?"

"Yes. All my cosmetics."

"Your cosmetics?"

"All of them."

"What on earth are you talking about?"

"Come. I'll show you."

In the bathroom, she opened the medicine chest.

"This morning, that window was open, and all my cosmetics were missing."

The medicine chest was bare, as were other shelves in the bathroom.

"Only your cosmetics were missing?"

"Some aspirin. My toothpaste."

"Your towels are here."

"No. One towel is missing."

"One towel is missing. They must have used it to carry off the cosmetics."

"That's what I figure."

"Surely, Mrs. Faulkner, that window is not large enough for an adult."

"I wouldn't think so."

"Some child in the neighborhood must have broken in and stolen your cosmetics."

"I would say so."

"Probably afraid to venture farther into the apartment."

"I'm glad you're so busy protecting the morals of the children in this neighborhood, Mr. Whatever-your-name-is, Greene Brothers

Management. I'd hate to have them thinking dirty thoughts while they're in jail for burglary."

23

It was lunch time. The corridors of the *News-Tribune* were cool and empty.

Fletch dropped two wrapped sandwiches and a carton of milk on his desk and took off his suit jacket.

He picked up the phone and dialed the number of the managing editor.

"This is Fletcher. I want to talk to Frank."

"Are you in the office, Fletch?"

"Yes."

"He's at lunch. He'll be back at two o'clock. Can you wait till then?"

"I'll twiddle my thumbs. Please make sure I see him at two."

Fletch loosened his tie and sat down.

While eating the sandwiches, he found the subpoena. Ordered to appear in court Friday morning at ten o'clock. Failure to pay alimony to Barbara Ralton Fletcher. Contempt of court. Failure to appear will cause instant arrest.

"Jesus Christ."

Friday morning he had the choice of receiving a Bronze Star and thus being arrested, or facing contempt charges in court and thus being fired.

"Jesus Christ."

The phone rang.

"Hello, for Christ's sake."

"Is this Mr. Fletcher?"

"If you insist."

"What?"

"Who is this?"

"This is Mr. Gillett, of Gillett, Worsham and O'Brien."

128

"Jesus Christ."

"Mr. Fletcher, I regret to tell you that the check you gave me the other day as payment of back and present alimony to Mrs. Linda Fletcher, in the amount of three thousand, four hundred and twenty-nine dollars, is no good."

"You bastard. I asked you not to cash it for ten days."

"I didn't try to cash it, Mr. Fletcher. However, I did take the precaution of making an inquiry at the bank. You don't even have an account in that bank, Mr. Fletcher."

"What?"

"You do not now, you never have had an account in the Merchants Bank. Not a checking account, not a savings account. Nothing."

"Nice of you to tell me."

"Where did you get that check, Mr. Fletcher?"

"I'm sorry, I didn't hear you. I was clearing my throat."

"It doesn't matter. What does matter is that I warned you when we met in your office last Friday that if you didn't play straight with us from now on, I would lower the boom on you. I would bring you back to court. You have provided me with ample opportunity for doing precisely that."

"Mr. Gillett—"

"You listen to me. This morning I have gone into court and seen to it that contempt charges are filed against you. A subpoena ordering you to appear in court Friday morning at ten o'clock will arrive within minutes."

"No."

"What do you mean, 'No'?"

"I can't be there Friday morning."

"Why not?"

"I've already been subpoenaed to appear in court Friday morning at ten o'clock to answer contempt charges for not paying alimony to my first wife, Barbara."

"Mr. Fletcher, I can't care about that."

"Well, I can't be in two places at the same time."

"At least we know Friday morning you will not be before a justice of the peace getting married again."

"Anyway, Friday morning at ten o'clock I'm also supposed to be in the marine commandant's office receiving a Bronze Star."

"Really, Mr. Fletcher. I've had enough of your stories."

"It's true. If I don't pick up the damned Bronze Star, I'll get fired. Then where will all my wives be?"

"They'll still be in court, Mr. Fletcher, hopefully represented by able attorneys."

"Jesus."

"What's more, Mr. Fletcher, in further implementation of my threat to lower the boom on you, this morning I also filed criminal charges against you for fraud."

"Fraud?"

"Fraud, Mr. Fletcher. It is against the law, Mr. Fletcher, to present checks against bank accounts that don't exist."

"How can you do this to me?"

"I'm obliged to. As an attorney practicing law in the state of California, I am an officer of the court, and I would be derelict in my duty to know that a crime has been committed without reporting it to the authorities."

"You reported me. Criminal charges."

"I was obliged to, Mr. Fletcher."

"You just bit the hand that feeds you. How can I support my ex-wives if I'm in jail?"

"I have bitten the hand which has refused to feed us. You haven't yet supported your ex-wives."

"Mr. Gillett."

"Yes, Mr. Fletcher?"

"I wonder if you and I might not meet in some quiet, out-of-the-way place, a bar, or take a ride in the country, spend a night or two. . ."

"Are you serious?"

"Of course I'm serious."

"I think that's a delightful idea. I don't know how you guessed, but I am rather attracted to you, Mr. Fletcher. But I really think we had better put these legal matters behind us first, don't you?"

130

"I was thinking this might be a very good way of putting our legal matters behind us."

"Your legal problems, Mr. Fletcher, are between you and your wives. And now, of course, a criminal court. Any relationship you and I might have should have nothing to do with your legal matters."

"Are you sure?"

"Mr. Fletcher. Are you pulling my leg?"

"That's what I'm pulling. Yes."

Gillett breathed three times before speaking again.

"Mr. Fletcher, I don't know whether you are a very, very cruel boy, or just thoroughly confused. I would prefer to think the latter. I am a member of the Anglican faith. If you are confused, I would be extremely pleased to continue our relationship more affectionately at some future time. For the moment, however, I advise you that a subpoena to face contempt of court charges Friday morning is immediately forthcoming. And I also advise you that criminal charges for fraud have been filed against you, and, although I am not your attorney, I would suggest to you that you present yourself at the main police station this afternoon, identify yourself, and allow yourself to be arrested. This should permit you to be out on bail in time for your other court appearances Friday morning."

"Thank you very much, Mr. Gillett. See you in church."

Fletch was chewing the second half of his first sandwich, feeling guilty about what he had done to Sandra Faulkner, when the phone rang again.

"Hello?"

"Fletch? This is Barbara."

"Barbara, my first wife?"

"I've been calling you every half hour for days. I was hoping to talk to you before the subpoena arrived."

"I'm having it for lunch."

"I'm sorry about that, Fletcher."

"Tut, tut, my dear. Think nothing of it. What's a little contempt of court charge between old friends?"

131

"It's the lawyers who are doing it, Fletch. They insist. They are real worried about the eight thousand dollars you owe me."

"Is it that much?"

"Eight thousand four hundred twelve dollars."

"Golly. I should have taken care of that. How careless of me."

"It really isn't my fault, Fletch. I mean the contempt of court thing. I didn't do it."

"Not to worry, Barbara. A little enough matter. Easy to straighten out. I'll pop down to court Friday morning and straighten things out in a switch of a lamb's tail."

"You're wonderful, Fletcher."

"Tut tut."

"I mean, it's not the money I care about, or anything. I know how much you earn from the newspaper. You can't afford it."

"I understand precisely."

"You do?"

"Certainly, Barbara."

"Fletcher, I'm still in love with you."

"I know. Isn't it awful?"

"It's been two years."

"That long?"

"I never even see you around town anymore. I've put on weight."

"You have?"

"I've been eating too much. I heard you got married again and divorced again."

"Just a temporary defection from my one true love."

"Really? Why did you get married again?"

"It came over me one day. With chills and prickly heat."

"Why did you get divorced?"

"Well, Barbara, it came down to a question between the cat and me. One of us had to go. The cat went first."

"I didn't call you all the time you were married."

"Thank you."

"I just heard you got divorced last week. I bumped into Charlie."

"How's Charlie?"

"Fletcher, do you think you and I could make it together again?"

132

"How much weight did you say you've gained?"

"A lot. I'm really gross."

"I'm sorry to hear that."

"I don't like the place I'm living. Are you still in the apartment on Clearwater Street?"

"I still live on the Street of Magnificent Plumbing."

"I'm sorry I divorced you, Fletch. I really regret it."

"Ah, well. Easy come. Easy go."

"That's not funny."

"I'm trying to eat a sandwich."

"What I'm trying to say is, I'm trying to apologize to you. For divorcing you."

"Don't give it a thought."

"I've grown up a lot."

"It comes with gaining weight, I think."

"The girls really bothered me, you know."

"Girls? What girls?"

"Oh, Fletch. You were just making love to everybody in town. All the time. You'd be gone for days on end. Sometimes I think you were making love to five or six different girls a week. I mean, you never hesitated."

"I get seduced easily."

"I thought it was awful. Every girl I looked at on the street, complete strangers, their eyes would say: I've made love to your husband, too. It was spooky. I mean, you never hesitated to make love to anybody."

"It's good exercise."

"Anyway, I think I've grown up. To accept that."

"You have?"

"Yes, Fletch. I understand. You're a male nymphomaniac."

"I am not."

"You are, Fletch. You just run around the city fucking people."

"Well . . ."

"You can't deny it."

"Well . . ."

133

"I think it's cute. I can accept it, now. You do understand that at first it bothered me."

"I don't know why it should."

"It did. But it won't anymore. I'm all grown up now, and you can play with anybody you like."

Fletch drank from the carton of milk.

"Fletch?"

"Yes, Barbara?"

"What I mean is: can we live together again?"

"What a wonderful idea."

"Are you serious?"

"Sure, Barbara."

"My lease runs out the end of this week—"

"Move in Friday."

"Really?"

"Friday morning. Sorry I won't be able to help you, but as you know, I have to run down to court for a few minutes."

"I know. How awful."

"But it would make everything all right, if you're there at the apartment when I get back."

"I've got a lot of junk now. I'll need a whole moving van."

"That's all right. You just back the moving van up to the service elevator and get yourself moved in. Arrange things as you like. And then when I get back from court, we'll have a nice lunch together."

"Terrific. Fletcher, you're beautiful."

"Just like the old days, Barbara."

"I'd better get packing."

"See you Friday. Maybe I'll take the weekend off."

"Fletcher, I love you."

As Fletch was reaching for the second half of the second sandwich, the phone rang again. It was almost two o'clock.

"I.M. Fletcher's line."

"Fletcher, that's you."

"Linda—my second wife."

"What happened to you the other night?"

"What other night?"

"Friday night. You told me to rush right over. To the apartment. You weren't there."

"I got held up."

"It wasn't funny, Fletcher. I mean, if that's your idea of a joke."

"Are you sore?"

"Of course not. At your apartment, I got all ready. I washed my hair and everything. It took me a while to find the dryer. The hair dryer."

"You washed your hair?"

"And I waited and I waited. I slept on the couch."

"Poor Linda."

"It wasn't very funny."

"I told you I was stoned."

"What happened to you."

"I ended up at The Beach."

"Couldn't you have waited for me?"

"I didn't know I was going."

"Did you spend the night with a girl?"

"Yes."

"You're something else."

"Linda, I've been thinking . . ."

"Doesn't sound it."

"I mean, since the other night. I had to go think."

"I understand. You always had to go think."

"I've been thinking about you since the other night. What I mean is, you know, I don't earn much here on the newspaper."

"I know. By the way, Mr. Gillett says there was something funny about your check."

"I know. He has me in court Friday morning."

"Poor Fletch."

"I agree. We must do something, Linda."

"Like what?"

"Well, I mean, I'm not earning much, and you've lost your job at the boutique, and it just doesn't make sense for us to be running two apartments."

135

"We're divorced."

"Who cares about that? You wanted to move back in last Friday night."

"I still do."

"So why don't you? Give up your apartment, and move in?"

"I want to."

"So okay. Do it."

"When?"

"Friday morning. That way we can spend the weekend together."

"You mean, move in permanently?"

"I mean, give up your apartment, get a moving van, and move your junk back into our apartment Friday morning, put everything away, arrange things as you like, and be there when I get back from court."

"Really?"

"Really. Will you do it?"

"Sure. That's a wonderful idea."

"I think it makes great sense, don't you?"

"I hate this place I'm living in, anyway."

"Maybe you'll even have lunch ready when I get back. Maybe we'll go to The Beach for the weekend."

"Wonderful idea. I really do love you, Fletch."

"Me, too. I mean, I love you, too. See you Friday."

24

"Clara Snow is an incompetent idiot. She knows nothing about this business. She is too stupid to learn."

Frank Jaffe, editor-in-chief of the *News-Tribune*, was sober only a few moments a day. Two o'clock in the afternoon was not one of those moments. At nine in the morning he was bleary-eyed and hung over. At eleven he was reasonable, but also reasonably nervous: he saw everyone as being in the way between him and his first luncheon martini. At eleven-thirty he would dash through the city room to commence drinking his lunch. From two to four-thirty he was coherently drunk. At five he was impatient, irascible. Evening drinking began at six. By nine he was incoherently drunk. In the evening he would phone the office frequently shouting orders no one could ever understand. He would spend much of the next day countermanding the orders he could remember which nobody had understood anyway. From the editor-in-chief's office would flow daily a sheaf of oblique "clarifications" which disturbed everyone and made no sense to anyone.

Fletch wondered how he had the energy for Clara Snow.

From across his oak desk, Frank's eyes behind glasses appeared to be trying to focus on him from the bottom of a jar of clam juice.

"What?"

"Clara Snow is an incompetent idiot. She knows nothing about newspapering. She is so stupid she can't learn."

"She's your boss."

"She is an incompetent idiot. She almost got me killed. She might yet."

"What did she do?"

"I've been working on this drugs-on-the-beach story—"

"For too goddamn long a time, too."

"Clara Snow reported to the chief of police at The Beach that I was there on an investigation and getting close to something."

"What's wrong with that? You might need police protection."

"What's wrong with it is that I believe the chief of police is the source of the drugs on the beach."

"You're kidding."

"I'm not kidding."

"Chief Graham Cummings? I've known him for ten years. Fifteen years. He's a wonderful man."

"He's the drug source."

"The hell he is."

"The hell he isn't."

Frank found it difficult to focus on people. "Fletcher, I think I'm taking you off this assignment."

"The hell you are."

"You've spent too goddamn long at it, and you've come up with nothing. You've just been horsing around at The Beach."

"If you take me off it, Frank, I will write it for the *Chronicle-Gazette* and publish it with the statement that you refused to publish it."

"We've been knockin' the police too hard lately."

"Graham Cummings is a drug source."

"What evidence do you have?"

"I'll write it."

"You have no evidence."

"Besides that, he's thrown me out of town. If I had been honest with him this morning and told him I have evidence, I think he would have killed me. If he gets one whiff of the evidence, he will kill me. I asked Clara Snow not to call the police."

"And Clara asked me and I said 'Go ahead.' "

"It was a damn-fool thing to do, Frank. When a man's on a story, he knows what he's doing. If I had wanted police protection, I would have sought it. It is not for you guys, you or Clara, to sit back here, setting me up as a clay pigeon."

"Did you tell Clara you suspected Cummings?"

"No. Because when I was talking to her last Friday I didn't suspect Cummings."

"So what are you saying?"

Frank looked like an unhappy frog sitting on a pad. As what Fletch was saying went through his mind, his chest expanded, his cheeks expanded and his eyes widened. His face became red.

He turned his swivel chair sideways to his desk. That way he didn't have to look at Fletch at all.

"Look, Fletcher, you and I have quite a bit to talk about. Clara says you've been pretty obnoxious. She says you dress like a slob, never wear shoes in the office, never answer your telephone, that she never knows where you are, that you're not working very hard, not working at all, that you don't accept editing, that you're sort of rude. . . . She says you're insubordinate and disobedient."

"Gee, boss, no wonder she set me up to be murdered."

"You're being rude now. Clara didn't know she was setting you up to be murdered, and I don't believe it yet. Graham Cummings is a decent guy."

"You have me saying Clara's an idiot, and Clara saying I'm an idiot. Doesn't that lead you to some conclusion?"

"What conclusion?"

"Separate us. If you insist on her being an editor, let her go make someone else's life miserable."

"I won't do that. You'll live with her."

"No. You live with her."

Frank's full face snapped to Fletcher. He tried to glare. Instead, his face just turned redder.

Frank said, "You're hanging on here by a thread now, boy."

"I sell newspapers."

"If it weren't that you're scheduled to pick up a Bronze Star Friday, I'd fire you in a minute."

"What I'm really saying, Frank, is that I am on a story, an investigation of the source of the drugs at The Beach. I'm not being dramatic, but I might be killed. If I am killed, some superior ought to know why. I believe the chief of police at The Beach, Graham Cummings, is the source. Clara Snow has tipped him off that I am on his heels. This morning he called me in to ask me what I know. This was after I tried to get arrested Sunday night. I tried very hard to get arrested. I belted three cops, in the chief's presence. I got a crack on the head, but I did not get arrested. This morning I played dumb. Very, very dumb. I told him I know nothing but the obvious. He told me to get out of town. It's reasonable to expect that if he begins to believe I've got hard evidence on him, he might want to kill me. You and your incompetent idiotic Clara Snow will have killed me."

"You're dramatizing yourself."

"Maybe."

"So what are you saying? You don't want to finish the story?"

"I'll finish it."

"When will you have it finished?"

"Pretty soon."

"I want to see it."

"You'll see it."

"You'd better pick up the Bronze Star Friday morning."

"By all means, Frank. Have reporters and photographers there. I look forward to having my face splashed all over the newspaper Saturday morning. That would surely get me killed."

"You collect that medal."

"Definitely, Frank. Friday morning, ten o'clock, the marine commandant's office."

"You pick up that medal, Fletcher, or Friday's will be your last paycheck."

"I wouldn't think of disappointing you, Frank."

"By the way, Clara also says you've got sleazy divorce lawyers all over this office. Keep them out of here."

"Right, Frank."

Fletch stood up and changed his tone of voice entirely. "What do you think of Alan Stanwyk?"

"He's a shit."

"Why?"

Frank said, "Stanwyk has fought every sensible piece of noise pollution legislation brought up in the last five years."

"And he's won?"

"Yes, he's won."

"What else do you know about him?"

"Nothing. He's a shit. Go get killed. Then maybe we'd have a story."

"Thanks, Frank."

"Anytime."

25

"Good afternoon, sir." The headwaiter recognized him, even dressed in a full suit. The man was wasted on a tennis pavilion. "Are you looking for the Underwoods?"

"Actually, I'm looking for Joan Stanwyk," Fletch said.

"Mrs. Stanwyk is playing tennis, sir. Court three. There's an empty table at the rail. Shall I have a screwdriver brought to you?"

"Thank you."

Fletch sat at the round table for two. Along the rail were flower boxes. In the third court away from Fletch, Joan Stanwyk was playing singles with another woman.

"Your screwdriver, sir. Shall I charge this to the Underwoods?"

"Please."

Half of court three was in the shade of the clubhouse. This made serving difficult half the time for both players. One would think Joan Collins Stanwyk could get a better court at the Racquets Club.

Half the people on the tennis pavilion were still dressed in tennis whites. The other half were dressed for the evening. It was five-twenty.

Joan Collins Stanwyk played tennis like a pro, but utterly without the flash of passion that made a champion. She was smooth, even, polished; a well-educated, well-experienced tennis player. It was difficult to get anything by her, or to outthink her, yet she didn't seem to be deeply involved—paying attention. She was also without the sense of fun and of joy that a beginning tennis player has. She was competent, terrifically competent, and bored.

She won the set, walked to the net, shook hands with her opponent and smiled precisely as she would have if she had lost. They both collected sweaters and ambled up to the pavilion.

Fletch turned his chair to face the entrance.

She had to greet many people, using the same shake of the hand and smile as she used at the net. It was a moment before her eyes wandered along the rail and found Fletch.

He stood up.

She excused herself and came over immediately.

"Why, John. I thought you were in Milwaukee."

"Montana," Fletch said.

"Yes, of course. Montana." She sat at the table.

"Just before leaving for the airport Saturday, my boss called and asked me to stay a few more days. Some customers to see."

141

"Why didn't you call me?"

"I was busy seeing customers." He was sitting at the table, finishing his drink. "Besides, I thought I would come by on Tuesday."

"Why Tuesday?"

"Because you said Tuesday was the day your husband came home from the office at a reasonable hour."

Beneath her tan, her cheeks turned red.

"I see."

"Didn't you say your husband has Tuesdays reserved for you?"

"You're rather putting it to me, aren't you, John?"

"I hope to."

Joan Collins Stanwyk, keeping her eyes in his, laughed. She had a lovely throat.

She said, "Well, now. . ."

He said, "I'm sorry I can't offer you a drink."

"You ask a great many more questions than you appear to ask, John. And what's more, you listen to the answers. You must be very good at what you do."

"What do I do?"

"Why, sell furniture, of course. Isn't that what you said?"

"I'm really quite expert on beds."

She said, "Would you believe that I have one?"

She had one, at the Racquets Club, a three-quarter-sized bed in a bright room overlooking the pool area. She said it was her "changing room." It had a full bathroom and a closet full of tennis dresses, evening gowns, skirts, sneakers and shoes.

She had given him directions to the door on the corridor above the dining room.

By the time he arrived, she was out of the shower and wrapped in an oversized towel.

Joan Collins Stanwyk was more interested in making love than in playing tennis. But again, she was educated and experienced without the flash that makes champions. And she was without the playful joy of the beginner.

142

"It's really remarkable, John."

"Isn't it?"

"That's not what I mean."

"What's remarkable?"

"Your bone structure."

"I have one."

"One what?"

"One bone structure. I'm very attached to it."

"I should think you would be."

"Yes, yes."

"But you never noticed."

"Never noticed what?"

"Never in the showers in Texas, or whatever."

"It's been a long time since I took a shower in Texas."

"Al's bone structure."

"Al's bone structure? What about it?"

"It's identical to yours."

"My what?"

"Your bone structure."

"What do you mean?"

"I mean the width of your shoulders, the length of your back, your arms, your hips, your legs are identical to Alan's."

"Your husband's?"

"Yes. Didn't you ever notice? You must have been in shower rooms with him in Texas, or something. The shape of your head—everything."

"Really?"

"You two don't look a bit alike. You're blond and he's dark. But actually you're just alike."

"Something only a wife would notice."

"He weighs ten or twelve pounds more than you do, I'd say. But your bone structures are the same."

"That's very interesting."

She rolled onto her elbows and forearms, looking closely at his mouth.

"Your teeth are perfect, too. Just like Alan's."

"They are?"

"I'll bet you haven't a cavity."

"I haven't."

"Neither has he."

"How very interesting."

She said, "Now I bet you're insulted."

"Not a bit."

"I don't suppose it's polite to compare you to my husband just after we've made love and made love."

"I find it interesting."

"You're saying to yourself, 'The only reason this broad was attracted to me is because I have the same bone structure as her husband.' Is that right?"

"Yeah. Actually, I'm terribly hurt."

"I didn't mean to hurt you."

"I'm going to cry."

"Please don't cry."

"I'm dying of a broken heart."

"Oh, don't die. Not here."

"Why 'not here'?"

"Because if I had to have your body taken away, I'd be absolutely stuck trying to pronounce your last name. I'd be so embarrassed."

"Is it embarrassing being in bed with a man whose last name you can't pronounce?"

"It would be if he died and had to be taken away. I'd have to say at the door, 'His name is John, an old friend of the family, don't ask me his last name.' What is your last name again, John?"

"Zamanawinkeraleski."

"God, what a moniker. Zamanawink—say it again?"

"—eraleski. Zamanawinkeraleski."

"You mean someone actually married you with a name like that?"

"Yup. And now there are three little Zamanawinkeraleskis."

"What was her maiden name? I mean, your wife's?"

"Fletcher."

"That's a nice name. Why would she give up a nice name like that to become a Zamabangi or whatever it is?"

144

"Zamanawinkeraleski. It's more distinguished than Fletcher."

"It's so distinguished no one can say it. What is it, Polish?"

"Rumanian."

"I didn't know there was a difference."

"Only Poles and Rumanians care about the difference."

"What is the difference?"

"Between Poles and Rumanians? They make love differently."

"Oh?"

"Twice I've made love Polish style. Now I'll show you how a Rumanian would do it."

"Polish style was all right."

"But you haven't seen the Rumanian style yet."

"Why didn't you make love Rumanian style in the first place?"

"I didn't think you were ready for it."

"I'm ready for it."

It was eight-thirty.

In forty-eight hours Fletch was scheduled to murder her husband.

26

Wednesday morning, Fletch had a great interest in not being seen by the police at The Beach. Doubtless, Chief Cummings had told his officers to pick up Fletch on sight. The man could not bear investigation. And he had enough ammunition to use against Fletch to make life very difficult for him. Possession of marijuana. Possession of heroin. Physical assault upon three separate police officers. And when Chief Cummings ran out of charges at The Beach, he could turn Fletch over to the city police to face a charge of fraud. Fletch was careful in his stepping.

In jeans, shoeless and shirtless, he started shortly after sunrise looking for Gummy.

It was a quarter to nine when July said he had just seen Gummy parking a Volkswagen minibus on Main Street.

145

Fletch found the flower-decorated bus and waited in the shadow of a doorway.

At twenty to ten Gummy appeared. While he had been waiting, Fletch had counted five police cars passing on Main Street.

Gummy was unlocking the driver's door to the bus.

Fletch stepped beside him and said, "Take me around to my pad, will you, Gummy? I need to talk to you."

Gummy's face pimples twitched.

"Come on, Gummy. I've got to talk to you. About Bobbi."

In the room, Fletch said, "Bobbi's dead, Gummy."

Gummy said, "Oh."

Fletch smashed him in the face with his fist.

Gummy's head snapped back and turned, his long hair twirling. His feet moved slowly. He did not fall. He turned back, his head low, looking at Fletch through watering eyes. The look was resentful. The kid had never been hit before.

"I said Bobbi is dead, Gummy, and 'Oh' is not a proper response. You killed her. And you know it."

Gummy stepped toward the door.

Fletch said, "I've got bad news for you, Gummy. Bobbi's death means the heat's on. Fat Sam is turning state's evidence."

"Bullshit."

"He has written me a nice little deposition naming Chief Graham Cummings as the source. Everything is in the deposition, including your Hawaiian shirt. He's pinning the actual sale of drugs on you. He insists he was just a receiver."

The kid had stopped moving toward the door. His eyes were wide and innocent.

"I never pushed. I was just carrying."

"You were transferring, baby."

Gummy had blood at the corner of his lip.

"I never sold any of the stuff."

"Fat Sam is laying it on you."

"The bastard."

146

"And he has signed the deposition in big, flowing handwriting with his real name—which I forget for the moment."

"Charles Witherspoon."

"What?"

"Charles Witherspoon."

"That's right."

"Where is this what-do-you-call-it?"

"Deposition. I left it in the city. Do you think I'd be crazy enough to bring it down here? He signed it Charles Witherspoon."

"Shit."

"Let me help you, Gummy." Fletch opened the case of his portable typewriter. He placed an original and two carbon sheets in the carriage. "You need help."

Gummy stood in the dark room with his hands in his back pockets.

"By the way, Gummy, I'm I.M. Fletcher of the *News-Tribune*."

"You're a reporter?"

"Yeah."

"I knew there was something funny about you. I saw you riding in a gray Jaguar last week—I think Thursday night."

"Did you tell anybody you saw me?"

"No."

Gummy sat on the floor. He leaned his back against the wall.

"Does this mean I go to jail?"

"Maybe not, if you turn state's evidence."

"What does that mean? I fink?"

"It means you write a deposition and sign it. You say what role you played in supplying the beach people with drugs."

"I carried the drugs from the chief of police to Fat Sam."

Fletch was sitting on the floor cross-legged before his typewriter.

"You've got to tell us more than that. Tell me everything. I'll write it down. And you sign it."

"You know everything."

"I need to hear it from you."

"What are you going to do with the deposition?"

"I'm going to turn it over to a friend of mine who works in the district attorney's office. We were in the marines together. He'll know what to do."

"I'll get killed. Cummings is a mean son of a bitch."

"I'm going to ask for police protection for you."

" 'Police protection'? That's funny."

"Not the local police, Gummy. I agree Cummings is a dangerous man."

"Who then? The state police?"

"Probably federal narcotics agents. Or the district attorney's office. I don't know. You'll be taken care of. I want you to nail Cummings."

"All right." The light from the dirty window was white on Gummy's long face. "Cummings was the source of drugs."

"All the drugs?"

"Yes. All."

"What is his source?"

"I don't know. He goes back and forth to Mexico every few weeks. He tells people he's building a house down there, or something. For when he retires. He brings the drugs back with him. No one questions the chief of police going through customs."

"How does customs know he's a police chief?"

"Aw, hell, have you ever seen his car? I mean, his own car? Plates front and back say 'chief of police.' He has a bubble machine on top. A police radio. He even has a Winchester rifle hanging from brackets under his dashboard."

"I've seen it. He uses that car to get through customs?"

"Yes."

"Does he wear his uniform going through customs?"

"I don't know. I've never been with him. With that car, he doesn't need a uniform."

"Does he take his wife to Mexico with him?"

"I know he has. And his teenage daughter."

"How do you know he has?"

"I've seen them leaving town. When I've known where they were going."

"Okay, Gummy. Now tell me how you get the drugs."

"Every week or ten days, they arrest me. They pull me down to the station house for questioning."

"Who picks you up?"

"Town police. Two of them, if I'm alone on the street. If I'm with you guys, I mean the guys on the beach, they send more. Like Sunday. There were seven of them. All dressed for a riot. They always expect somebody to jump on them. Like you did Sunday. By the way, Fletch, why did you do that Sunday?"

"I wanted to get arrested. I wanted to go to the station house with you and see precisely what happened."

"They really cracked your head. It sounded like a gunshot."

"It did to me, too. Is Chief Cummings always with the cops who pick you up?"

"No. But they always say the chief wants me for questioning. They're a stupid bunch of cops."

"What happens when you get to the station house?"

"I wait in the chief's office. He comes in and closes the door. He pretends to question me. I give him the money, he gives me the drugs. As simple as that. Sometimes they keep me in a jail cell over night. It looks better."

"How does the chief know that it's time to pick you up—that you're carrying money for him?"

"I park the minibus so he can see it from his office window."

"How much money do you turn over to him, on the average?"

"It averages about twenty thousand bucks."

"Every two or three weeks?"

"Every ten days or so."

"How do you transfer the money?"

"You said Fat Sam's already told you."

"I want to hear it from you."

"In a money belt. Under my Hawaiian shirt."

"And that's how you bring the drugs to Fat Sam?"

"Yeah. I carry the drugs in the money belt under the Hawaiian shirt."

"How do you actually give it to Fat Sam?"

"I don't. I just walk to the back of the lean-to and drop it. He knows where to pick it up. Then I line up like everyone else and make a phony cash buy."

"I've seen that. You really fooled me. So what do you get out of this?"

"Free drugs. Like the man said, all I can eat."

"No cash?"

"No cash. Never."

"How did you pay for the minibus?"

"That belongs to Fat Sam. You should know that. Didn't he tell you that?"

"No, he didn't. I've never seen him use it."

"He never leaves the beach."

"Why does he never leave the beach?"

"He's afraid someone would try to rip him off. Everyone thinks he's carrying. Either drugs or money. He's not, of course. I am."

"How does he give you the money?"

"In the money belt. I pretend to buy drugs every few days. When I see the money belt rolled up at the back of the lean-to, I sit down and put it on under my shirt."

"Okay, Gummy. You're doin' fine."

"Yeah."

"When Chief Cummings takes the money and gives you the drugs, are you always in the room alone with him?"

"Yes. With the door shut."

"Has there ever been another police officer or anyone else with you at the transfer of the drugs and money?"

"No. Never."

"Do you think any of the other police officers know that the chief is the source of the drugs at The Beach?"

"They're dumb bunnies. None of them know. None of them have ever figured it out."

"Aren't they suspicious that you, and only you, are brought in for questioning every week or ten days?"

"My Dad's superintendent of schools. They think Cummings has a particular concern for me. I also think they think I'm informing.

I suspect some of them even think I'm working for the chief, as a spy."

"How long has this routine been going on?"

"How many years?"

"Yeah. How many years?"

"About four years."

"How old are you, Gummy?"

"Seventeen."

"So you couldn't have been using the minibus as a signal to the chief originally. What were you using?"

"My bicycle. I'd chain it to a parking meter: He'd be able to see it through his office window. My bike had a purple banana seat and a high rear-view mirror."

"How did you get started being the go-between?"

"I got hooked my first year in high school. The runner was a senior named Jeff. He blew his brains out with a shotgun. I didn't know he had been the runner until next time I went to Fat Sam."

"Was it Fat Sam who got you going?"

"No. The day after I was turned off I was pretty uptight, you know, pretty nervous. It was all beginning to hang out. In fact, I don't think I had really known I was hooked until that day. Until Jeff killed himself and the supply turned off. A couple of cops met me at the bicycle rack, at the school. They picked me up and brought me to the station. I was scared shitless. The chief closed the door to his office, and we had our first talk. We made our first deal."

"It was the chief who first got you going?"

"Yes."

"Was it Fat Sam who gave you your first drugs?"

"No. It was Jeff. At the high school. He got his free. He had extra. He gave it to me. I guess, seeing I was the son of the superintendent, they figured getting me hooked would give them some extra protection. At least regarding the drugs in the school. After a few months, Jeff stopped giving it to me free and sent me to Fat Sam. He said I wanted too much. For a while, until Jeff blew his brains out, I had to pay for it."

"How did you pay for it?"

"I burglarized my parents' house three times."

"Your own house?"

"Yeah. I was afraid to burglarize anyone else's. I was just a little kid. I really hated stealing the color television."

"Did your parents ever suspect you?"

"No. They would just report the burglary to Chief Cummings. Buy new stuff with the insurance money."

"Do your parents know you are a drug addict?"

"Yes. I guess so."

"Have they never talked to you about it?"

"No. Dad doesn't want to make an issue out of it. After all, he's superintendent of schools."

"Okay, Gummy. Just sit there and let me type a minute."

Fletch typed almost a whole page, single-spaced. He had Gummy sign the three copies. Lewis Montgomery. He had the handwriting of a nine-year-old boy. Fletch witnessed the signature on each copy.

"Is Bobbi really dead?"

Fletch said: "Yes."

"She OD'd?"

"Yes."

"Shit, I'm sorry."

"So am I."

"It's time this whole scene broke up. You know what I mean?"

"Yeah."

"I mean, I've been wondering how it would stop. Jeff blew his brains out."

"I know."

"I do feel badly about Bobbi."

"I know."

Fletch put the third copy of the deposition folded into his back pocket. He put the typewriter back into its case.

Gummy said, "What will happen to me now?"

"Tomorrow morning at eleven o'clock, I want you to be waiting at the beer stand. Fat Sam will be waiting there with you. You'll be picked up. Probably by plainclothesmen. Until tomorrow at eleven o'clock, I want you to shut up."

152

"Okay. Then what will happen? What will the fuzz do to me?"

"They'll probably bring you to a hospital and check you in under another name."

"I've got to come down, huh?"

"You want to, don't you?"

"Yes. I think so."

Fletch did not understand why Gummy did not leave. The boy remained sitting on the floor, his back against the wall, his face toward the window.

It was a moment before Fletch realized Gummy was crying.

Fletch walked into the lean-to carrying the typewriter.

Fat Sam was lying on his back on a bedroll on the sand, reading Marcuse's *Eros and Civilization*. The bedroll stank. Fat Sam stank.

"Hello, Vatsyayana."

In a back corner of the lean-to was a pile of empty soup cans. They stank.

Fletch handed Vatsyayana Gummy's deposition.

"I.M. Fletcher, of the *News-Tribune*."

Fat Sam put the book face-down on the sand.

While Fat Sam read the deposition, Fletch sat cross-legged on the sand and opened the portable typewriter case. Again he put an original and two carbons in the carriage.

Fat Sam read the deposition twice.

Then he sat up. His look remained kind.

"So."

"Your turn."

"You even have the name spelled right. Charles Witherspoon. It's been a long time since I've heard it."

"I guess Gummy got it from the registration of the Volkswagen."

"Oh, yes." Vatsyayana looked out at the sunlit beach. "You expect a deposition from me."

"I want to get Cummings."

"I don't blame you. A most unsavory man."

"Either you hang him, or you'll hang with him."

"Oh, I'll hang him all right. With pleasure."

Fat Sam reached for a book: Jonathan Eisen's *The Age of Rock*. In the back of the book was a folded piece of paper. Fat Sam blew the sand off it and handed it to Fletch. It read:

Sam—Jeff killed himself tonight. The boys investigating report of a gunshot found him on the football field. We need a new runner. Maybe the Montgomery kid. He may show up in the next day or two with the money belt. We need someone local.—Cummings.

"Is that hard evidence, or not?"

"That's hard evidence."

"Note, if you will, my dear Fletch, the gentleman wrote and signed it in his own hand."

"I do so note. How did you get it?"

"Would you believe it was delivered to me in a sealed envelope by an officer of the law? I've never known what to do with it. When there isn't the police, who is there? I forgot about the power of the press."

"You have wanted to turn Cummings in?"

"Always. I have been his prisoner, you see. Just as surely as if I were sitting in the town lock-up."

"I don't see."

"When I first came here from Colorado, I had a supply of drugs, thanks to my dear old mother's insurance. To support myself here, on this magnificent beach, I sold some of it off. The eminent chief of police had me arrested. He had the evidence. I either went to jail for a very long time, or worked for him. I chose not to go to jail."

"You mean you have never made a profit from this business?"

"No. Never. I have been a prisoner."

"Fat Sam, you're smarter than that. You're an intelligent man. You've known you could go over the head of the local police and turn Cummings in."

"You do realize, Fletch, that I am an addict, too?"

"Yes."

"I became addicted while teaching music in the Denver public school system. I was already at the end of my rope when my mother died, fortuitously leaving me fifteen thousand dollars in life insurance."

"You could have stopped the whole thing here anytime. Especially once you had this note."

"I realize that. The chief has continuously had evidence against me. Current evidence. Two, I am an addict. My profit from my partnership with the eminent chief of police has been free drugs all these years. Just like Gummy. The chief pays off only in merchandise. Three, I have always hoped for a guarantee of some sort, if I am to turn state's evidence. Do you have such a guarantee, Fletch?"

"Yes. I'll have you picked up at the beer stand tomorrow morning at eleven o'clock. You and Gummy."

"How very considerate of you. And then, I presume, you will splash this sordid affair all over your newspaper?"

"The whole story will be in tomorrow afternoon's *News-Tribune*. The first afternoon edition appears at eleven-twenty in the morning. If you are not at the beer stand at eleven, you will probably be dead by three o'clock in the afternoon."

"Oh, I'll be there. In fact, I would say you are pulling it rather close."

"I don't want to tip my hand until the morning."

"I see. And will you need photographs?"

"I have them already. Several fine shots of you, dealing. In fact, I had them developed and made yesterday at the office. They are awaiting captions."

"How very efficient. I remember once saying you weren't very bright. I think you are a very good actor."

"I'm a liar with a fantastic memory."

"That's what an actor is. How did you catch on?"

"I watched the drop three times before I realized it was Gummy. It was his Hawaiian shirt. It was his being picked up by the police regularly. He was the only one ever picked up by the police. And he was picked up only when your supply was running low. Actually, I think it was Creasey who mentioned the repetitious coincidence of timing. He didn't realize what he was saying. Then, Sunday night, when I tried to get arrested with Gummy and I belted three cops and they didn't arrest me, I knew Cummings did not want anyone with Gummy at the station. They wanted him alone."

"Of course."

"Then someone else mentioned the chief's frequent trips to Mexico. I heard that the first time last Saturday noon, from a very unlikely source."

"Who?"

"A man named John Collins."

"I don't know him."

"You don't play tennis."

"I used to. Back when I was alive. And how did you get the deposition out of Gummy?"

"I told him you had already signed one, naming him as pusher."

"That was dirty pool. And why would Gummy believe that I had signed a deposition?"

"Because Bobbi is dead, Fat Sam. She really is dead."

"I see. I'm sorry. She was a pretty child. Where is her body?"

"It's about to be found."

"And her body being found will trigger a whole chain of events. Supercops will flood The Beach."

"You wouldn't have a chance."

Fat Sam lit a joint and inhaled deeply. He handed it to Fletch.

"Peace."

"Fuck."

"That too."

Fletch inhaled twice.

"It's time," Fat Sam said. "It's time."

"Gummy said the same thing."

"I wonder if I have any life left. I am thirty-eight and feel one hundred."

"You'll get help."

"Now I wish they would put me in jail for a long time." Fat Sam inhaled again. "I suppose I don't really. I'm smoking a joint. I shot up two hours ago. Oh, Buddha."

"It's time to do the deposition."

"No, son. Move away from the typewriter. I'll do it myself."

156

Fletch lay down on the sand with the rest of the joint.

Fat Sam sat at the typewriter.

"Now let's see if Vatsyayana remembers how to type. Let's see if Fat Sam remembers how to type. Let's see if Charles Witherspoon remembers how to type."

To Fletch, stoned on the sand, the typing seemed very slow.

27

"It is Wednesday afternoon at three o'clock. Although I have what can be termed fresh intuitive evidence, I cannot pretend that I have much fresh factual evidence.

"My best guess at the moment, based on no factual evidence, is that Alan Stanwyk is absolutely straight—that what he says is the truth: he is dying of cancer; he wishes me to murder him tomorrow night at eight-thirty."

Fletch had returned to his apartment, taken a shower, eaten a sandwich and poured a quart of milk down his throat.

On the coffee table before him were the two depositions and their copies, and the original of Cummings's incriminating note to Fat Sam.

There was also the big tape recorder.

"Yesterday morning, Alan Stanwyk picked me up in his car again and confirmed my intention to murder him. We reviewed the murder plan.

"Conversationally, he asked me the flight number of the Trans World Airlines plane for Buenos Aires. I denied knowing the flight number, as he himself had not mentioned it to me. In fact, I did know the flight number, as I had confirmed the reservation with the airline.

"My apparent failure to know the flight number should have meant two things to him: first, he should continue seeing me in character, as a drifter—that is, I'm apparently as stupid and trusting as he thinks I am; second, he should be satisfied that if he is being investigated, I am not the source of the investigation.

"Conversationally, without appearing out of character, I was able to ask him one of my major questions: why, if he wishes to commit suicide, doesn't he crash in an airplane, as everybody half-expects?

"His answer was one of pride: that after years of keeping airplanes in the air, he couldn't aim one for the ground.

"This is an acceptable answer. As he pointed out, people do spend more than fifty thousand dollars in support of pride. Any man who lives in a house worth more than a million dollars can be expected to spend fifty grand on a matter such as this, which would so profoundly affect his most personal pride.

"Alan Stanwyk has a mistress, a Mrs. Sandra Faulkner, of 15641B Putnam Street. He spends Monday and Wednesday evenings with her.

"Mrs. Faulkner is a widow who used to work at Collins Aviation. Stanwyk and Mrs. Faulkner did not particularly know each other while Mrs. Faulkner worked at Collins Aviation.

"Sandra Faulkner's husband was a test pilot who was killed while attempting to land on an aircraft carrier, leaving her childless.

"At the time of the death, Sandra Faulkner left her employment at Collins Aviation, ran through her insurance money and whatever other sums she had available, and in the process became a drunk.

"It was approximately a year after the death that Alan Stanwyk discovered the straits she was in and came to her with what can only be described as a genuine instinct of mercy. Being a test pilot himself, it can be properly assumed his sympathy for the widow of a test pilot was entirely sincere.

"He paid for her hospitalization and has been supporting her ever since. I would estimate this affair has been going on about two years.

"Sandra Faulkner does not deny that she and Stanwyk have a sexual relationship.

"Joan Collins Stanwyk is unaware of the fact of this relationship, as she is quick to refer to her husband's working late at the office on Mondays and Wednesdays.

"However, I have subjective knowledge that Joan Collins Stanwyk herself is unfaithful to her husband.

"Returning to Sandra Faulkner: Stanwyk's mistress is unaware that Stanwyk is terminally ill, if he is. She is unaware of any change in the relationship in the foreseeable future, such as the possibility of sudden death.

"Her apartment and other belongings show no sign of being packed up.

"She is of the opinion that Stanwyk's health is excellent, and that their relationship will continue unchanged for the foreseeable future.

"Otherwise, I would characterize the relationship of Stanwyk and his mistress as generous on his part, even noble. Here is a woman of no great attraction, a heavy drinking and emotional problem, who desperately needs a friend. Stanwyk, really from a great distance, perceives that problem and becomes the friend she needs. He has no real reason to exercise such a sensitivity toward the widow of a man he never knew, or toward an unknown and unimportant ex-employee of Collins Aviation.

"Yet he does.

"This is the most consistently surprising element in Alan Stanwyk's character. The man has a peculiar principle and a unique sense of profound loyalty.

"Evidence of this rare personality trait can be found in his extraordinary, frequent, and reasonably secret trips to his hometown, Nonheagan, Pennsylvania, where his mother and father still live; in his refusing to join a fraternity at Colgate until the fraternity had made his roommate, Burt Eberhart, equally welcome; his subsequent loyalty to this same ex-roommate, Eberhart, in virtually setting him up in a business, supporting him royally as his personal and corporate insurance man, when the two men really have nothing in common at this point, if they ever did have; in his relationship with a mistress from which the mistress has benefited far more than he, and not just in worldly goods, but in mental, emotional and physical health.

"Despite Stanwyk's obvious personal ambition, which may be evidenced by his marrying the boss's daughter, which remains possible as a result of genuine love, as Amelia Shurcliffe pointed out, one really

159

must conclude that Alan Stanwyk is a remarkably decent and honest man. What he says is true.

"Nevertheless, I am professionally obliged to retain my skepticism to the ultimate moment.

"It is entirely possible I have not assembled the right facts, or noticed them, or put them in the right order. It is possible I have not asked the right questions.

"I must continue to believe that Stanwyk's basic statement, that he is dying of cancer, is not true until I have proved it true.

"So far I have not proved this basic statement true."

Fletch turned off the tape recorder and stood for a moment in front of the divan, studying the Disderi—four photographs of a dreadfully unattractive woman in nineteenth-century bathing costume. In it were so many truths: the truth of momentary fashion, the truth of what the woman thought of herself, thought of the experience of being photographed, the hard truth of the camera.

Fletch put down the microphone and rewound the Alan Stanwyk tape.

Wandering around the room, he listened to the tape, his own voice droning on, at first against a background of traffic noise, then in the silence of this same room, remembering that at first, less than a week ago, he wasn't sure who Alan Stanwyk was. The voice continued, not always succeeding in separating fact from speculation, observation from intuition, but nevertheless cutting through to a reasonable sketch of a man, his life and affairs: Alan Stanwyk.

Fletch played the tape again, going over the six days in his mind, trying to remember the smaller observations and impressions he had failed to record on the tape—clearly irrelevant matters. Joan Stanwyk was visibly lonely and drinking martinis before lunch on the Saturday her husband was flying an experimental airplane in Idaho. Dr. Joseph Devlin had answered the phone too fast when he heard the call concerned Alan Stanwyk—and he did not appear to question that the call had come from the insurance company. Sandra Faulkner's apartment had been burglarized, apparently by a child. Burt Eberhart thought Alan's daughter, Julie Stanwyk, a brat. Alan Stanwyk did not use the cigarette lighter on the dashboard of his car. He, Fletch, had not yet bought a pair of gloves. Fletch sat on the divan again and picked up the microphone.

"Alan Stanwyk is a decent man. A man of principle and profound loyalty. A strong man. An ambitious man.

"Everything in his life is intelligible and consistent—with one exception.

"I do not understand his relationship with his parents.

"He didn't invite his parents to his wedding. He hasn't told them they have a five- or six-year-old granddaughter.

"Yet he visits them across country every six weeks.

"The answer has to be that his relationship is not with his parents, but with Nonheagan, Pennsylvania."

Fletch turned off the tape recorder and went into the bedroom to use the phone.

It was four-thirty, Wednesday.

28

"Mr. Stanwyk? Believe it or not, this is Sidney James of Casewell Insurers again."

"I thought you'd call again. Once you long-distance dialers learn a telephone number, you're apt to ring it a lot."

"I expect this will be the last time I bother you, sir."

"That's all right, son. I hope it isn't. I bought some more telephone stock yesterday."

"The hardware store must be doing pretty well."

"It's doing all right. Ever since the price of labor went sky-high, people have been rushing to the hardware store to buy the wrong equipment for jobs around the house they never intend to do anyway. You've heard of selling used equipment? I bet half the stuff I sell never gets used in the first place."

"I thought you said the telephone company is the only business making money these days."

"The hardware business is doing pretty good, too. Although I'd only admit it long-distance to California."

"You seem to have things pretty well figured out, sir."

"How are you figuring these days? You picking up that Bronze Star?"

"Yes, sir, I am."

"That's good, son. That's fine. Can we keep it for you?"

"I noticed a space in the back of my sock drawer where I think it would fit."

"I thought you'd make the right decision. There never was a country that didn't need to decorate people."

"Thanks for the offer, anyway. How's Mrs. Stanwyk?"

"Oh, I forgot: you're a pulse-taker. When I was home for lunch, Mrs. Stanwyk was still ticking over nicely. The older models are the best, you know. Better built, and they use less fuel."

"Say, Mr. Stanwyk, the last time we talked you said your son, Alan, gave up boxing, refused to go to the nationals after winning the state's Golden Gloves, because of girls."

"Yes, I did say that."

"Is that what you meant?"

"Well, son, I believe a man of my age has sufficient motor memory to mean approximately the same thing when he says 'girls' as a young buck of your age. If I remember rightly, girls have a couple of legs under them, a hank o' hair up top, and a couple of protuberances about grab height. That about right?"

"That's about right, sir."

"I thought so."

"What I mean is, did you mean *girls*, or *girl?*"

"I'm in the hardware business, son. I'm apt to speak in gross lots."

"Did you mean any girl in particular? Was there any one particular girl who was the cause of Alan's giving up boxing?"

"There certainly was."

"Who was she?"

"You insurance men ask some funny questions."

"We'll be through with this case very soon, sir. We'll stop bothering you."

"Mr. James, you sound more like a private investigator or somethin' than an insurance man."

"Going over this policy, Mr. Stanwyk, we noticed a small bequest we don't understand. We have to check out whether the person is a relative or not, whether or not she is still alive, the current address, etc."

"I should think all that would be up to Alan, the insured."

"Your son's a very busy man, Mr. Stanwyk. You'd be surprised how people fail to maintain the proper information on policies of this sort."

"I suppose I would."

"They experience the death of a friend, or get a postcard saying a friend's address has changed, and it never occurs to them to update such a thing in an insurance file."

"I guess I understand. But if you hadn't won a Bronze Star, Mr. James, I think I'd be inclined to tell you to go leap into the Pacific Ocean. Are you near the Pacific Ocean out there?"

"I can see it through my window, Mr. Stanwyk. Who is the girl?"

"Sally Ann Cushing. Or, as she is now known, Sally Ann Cushing Cavanaugh."

"Alan and she were in love?"

"They were thicker than Elmer's Glue. Sticky. For years there, you hardly saw one without seeing the other one attached. If they weren't kissin', they were holdin' hands. Here in town we had to widen the sidewalks for them. You couldn't pry 'em apart."

"Alan gave up boxing because of Sally Ann Cushing?"

"As the old song says, 'Love walked in.' She set him on his ass like no long-armed middleweight ever did. He gave up boxing. He almost gave up everything, including breathing normally, for that girl. We had a hard time gettin' him to go to school."

"What happened?"

"Well, he went to Colgate and she went to Skidmore."

"They're reasonably close together, aren't they? I mean, as colleges?"

"Scandalously close. That's why the kids picked 'em. And every weekend they came home and continued being a sexual inspiration to us all. You never saw two kids so in love."

"So why didn't they get married?"

"They did, but not to each other. Spring of their senior year in college, Sally Ann was visibly pregnant. I do believe my wife noticed it before Alan. Naturally, we thought it was Alan. We thought it was Alan's kid. It wasn't. I guess their relationship had been as pure as the driven snow. Alan was shaken to his foundation. The kid was caused by a man named Bill Cavanaugh, a town boy. Sally Ann said that she had had too much to drink at a party here in town one night, while Alan was at school, and Cavanaugh had driven her home. She said he had taken advantage of her. She insisted it happened only once, but as Mother Goose said, once is enough. At least it was that time. Or, more likely, she wasn't telling the truth. I've always suspected she was a little impatient with my son. You know, Alan always played everything remarkably straight. There comes a time when a girl wants to get laid, and I suspect Alan was keeping the girl he intended to marry as untried as next year's car."

"So Sally Ann Cushing married Cavanaugh?"

"Yup. And Alan took up flying those damn-fool aircraft. Between the boxing and the flying, there was a hot and heavy romance with Sally Ann Cushing. Frankly, I think my son has always had a bit of a death urge. Although I suppose I shouldn't tell you that. Your bein' his insurance man. A bit of the daredevil, except when it came to young love. He treated that very carefully. A bit too carefully, I'd say."

"This explains a lot."

"Does this explain that small bequest on the insurance policy?"

"Yes. The name is Sally Ann Cushing Cavanaugh."

"That's good. She's a nice girl. I've always been a bit in love with her myself. Cavanaugh is a skunk, I've always thought. Never have liked him. The boy, young Bill, is about twelve years old now. One or the other frequently comes in the store, Sally Ann or young Bill. I feel toward them almost like family. Despite the pregnancy, Alan and Sally Ann still thought of getting married. But Cavanaugh had

164

his rights, and he exerted them. Sally Ann was quite a catch for him. He's in the insurance business, like you, only he's no good at it."

"The Cavanaughs still live in Nonheagan?"

"Well, yes and no. That's what I was going to tell you. I can't be too sure of Sally Ann's address at this point."

"Why not?"

"Sally Ann and Bill Cavanaugh got divorced a while back. I'm not sure exactly when. There was a separation. I know they were getting divorced, and she must have gotten it, because she sold her house and left town, taking the boy with her."

"When? When did she leave town?"

"Yesterday."

"Yesterday?"

"Yup. They sold everything. Furniture, washer, dryer, beds and kitchenware. There was no moving van at all. She and the boy packed suitcases and took a taxi to the airport. It's a bit of a mystery around here. According to my wife, they were very vague about where they were going. The kid said he was going to go live on the West Coast—out somewhere near you. In California. I expect that after almost thirteen years of marriage to that bum Cavanaugh, she just wanted to burn her bridges behind her. Find a new life somewhere. Anyway, be shut of this town. Cavanaugh gave her a pretty rough time."

"Mr. Stanwyk, thank you very much."

"Well, if there's any question about that little bequest to Sally Ann, you be a good fella and see that she gets what Alan wants to give her. Sally Ann is a wonderful person, and she's had a rotten time."

"One other question: when your son would visit you in Nonheagan, did he ever see Sally Ann?"

"Why, no. He was at the Inn on the telephone all the time, as far as I know. She was married. I suppose he could have seen her. He never mentioned it."

"Again, many thanks, Mr. Stanwyk. You've been a great help. We won't bother you again."

"Any time, Mr. James. I'm very happy to have the opportunity to help out Alan."

Fletch went through the routine with five local hotels before finding the right one.

"Desk, please."

"Desk."

"Has Mrs. Sally Ann Cavanaugh checked in yet?"

The sixth hotel desk answered, "Yes, sir. Mrs. Cavanaugh and her son checked in yesterday. Do you want their room number?"

"No. Thanks. We want to surprise her with some flowers. Can you tell me when she intends to check out?"

"She's keeping the room through Thursday night, sir, but she told us she would actually be leaving Thursday evening after supper. Tomorrow night about nine o'clock."

"That should give us plenty of time to send her flowers. Thanks very much."

"Trans World Airlines. Reservations."

"On your flight 629 to Buenos Aires tomorrow night," Fletch said, "do you have a reservation for a Mrs. Sally Ann Cushing Cavanaugh and son?"

"What's the name, sir?"

"Mrs. Cavanaugh and son, William."

"No, sir. We do not have reservations under that name. Should we make these reservations, sir?"

"No, no. That's all right. Do you have a reservation under the name of Irwin Fletcher for the same flight?"

"Irwin Fletcher. Yes, sir. Flight 629 to Buenos Aires. Departure time eleven P.M. Thursday. That reservation has been confirmed."

"And you do not have a Sally Ann Cushing Cavanaugh registered aboard that flight?"

"No, sir. We do not have either a Cushing or a Cavanaugh listed as passengers aboard flight 629."

Fletch said, "Thank you very much."

Before making the next telephone call, Fletch spent a few moments wandering around the apartment. In the kitchen he drank a glass of milk. In the bathroom he brushed his teeth. Back in the bedroom he spent a few minutes looking into the telephone directory.

Then he picked up the phone.

"Command Air Charter Service?"

"Yes. Hello. Command Air Charter Service."

"This is Irwin Fletcher. I'm calling regarding my reservation for tomorrow night . . ."

"Yes. Mr. Fletcher. We're glad you called. Your cashier's check arrived this morning, as we arranged. The flight is prepaid. An executive jet will be standing by tomorrow night from ten-thirty P.M. to twelve midnight for your flight to Rio de Janeiro. You don't expect to be arriving later than twelve midnight, do you, sir?"

"No. I don't. At the airport, aren't you right next to Trans World Airlines?"

"Yes, sir. We use the same parking facilities."

"I see."

"We haven't known where to call you, Mr. Fletcher, as you left no telephone number when we talked Friday of last week. You didn't indicate whether or not you'd be traveling alone, sir."

"No. Does it matter?"

"No, sir. Our only question is whether or not you wish a steward flying aboard."

"Is one usual?"

"Well, sir, if you're flying alone, the copilot usually can take care of such things as drinks and food . . ."

"I see."

"Will you wish a steward, sir? It makes no difference in cost to you. It just means one of our able stewards will be flying to Rio and back."

"Yes. I will want a steward."

"Yes, sir. That's fine. We'll have a steward on board."

"Thank you."

"Thank you, Mr. Fletcher. And thank you for calling in. This flight will not need to be confirmed again."

After replacing the telephone receiver, Fletch remained sitting on the bed. It was ten minutes past seven.

167

There were twenty-five hours and twenty minutes before he was next scheduled to meet Alan Stanwyk.

Fletch went over in his mind precisely what he had to do in that twenty-five hours and twenty minutes, and ordered the doing of these things in a time sequence. After making the plan, he adjusted it and then reviewed it.

There was plenty of time for what he had to do.

At seven-thirty Fletch fell asleep with his alarm set for one-thirty Thursday morning.

At three-twenty Thursday morning, Fletch parked his car on Berman Street, The Hills, three hundred yards from the Stanwyk driveway.

In sneakers and jeans and a dark turtleneck sweater, Fletch entered the Stanwyk property by the driveway. Leaving the driveway immediately, he approached the side of the house by walking in an arc across the left lawn.

He entered the library of the Stanwyk house by the french window. He reflected that it had even been true that the servants perpetually forgot to lock that door.

Using only moonlight, he slid open the top right drawer of the desk.

As he suspected, the .38 caliber Smith & Wesson revolver was still in the drawer.

And, as he had suspected, the bullet clip had been removed.

He returned the empty gun to the drawer.

At five-fifteen Thursday morning, Fletch was in his office at the *News-Tribune*, writing a story for Thursday afternoon's newspaper.

29

for 1st Thurs. p.m. BODY FOUND w/cuts: R. Sanders Fletcher

The nude body of a 15-year-old girl was discovered buried in the sand off Shoreside Blvd., The Beach, by police this morning.

The body was found encased in a sleeping bag in a shallow grave in the shade of the sea wall as the result of a tip from an anonymous caller.

The body has been identified as that of Roberta "Bobbi" Sanders, believed to be originally from Illinois.

It is expected that, in his report, coroner Alfred Wilson will estimate the time of death sometime late Sunday night or early Monday morning and the cause of death as an overdose of drugs.

According to a police spokesman, the sleeping bag is a popular brand and there is little expectation it can be traced to its owner.

The girl, abandoned at The Beach by a 30-year-old male traveling companion some months ago, had no known local address.

Her friends are not known to police.

She had no known means of support.

The anonymous caller this morning was described by police as "probably male." It is reported by the receiving officer that an obvious attempt was made by the caller to muffle or disguise the voice.

The Beach police are making every effort to locate the girl's family in Illinois.

It is believed her father is a dentist.

for 1st Thurs. p.m. (fp) POLICE CHIEF IMPLICATED Fletcher w/exhibits: 1) Montgomery affidavit; 2) Witherspoon affidavit; 3) Cummings's handwritten note— enclosed, captioned w/cuts: Cummings, Witherspoon, Montgomery—u have in rack.

The *News-Tribune* delivered to the district attorney's office this morning evidence implicating Chief of Police Graham Cummings in illegal drug trafficking in The Beach area.

The evidence includes: an affidavit signed by Charles Witherspoon, alias Vatsyayana, alias Fat Sam, who identifies himself in the affidavit as "the disseminator of [illegal] drugs in The Beach area," an affidavit signed by Lewis Montgomery, who identifies himself in the affidavit as "the drug runner to Fat Sam," and a handwritten note to "Sam" regarding drug-running problems signed "Cummings."

These affidavits identify Chief Cummings as the source of illegal drugs in The Beach area.

The affidavits are dated with yesterday's date.

This morning, The Beach police discovered the body of a 15-

year-old girl, Roberta "Bobbi" Sanders, buried in a shallow grave near the main sea wall at The Beach, dead of a drug overdose. (See related story.)

The evidence implicating Cummings is the result of a special investigation by the *News-Tribune* beginning a month ago.

Both Witherspoon and Montgomery were placed in protective custody before noon today.

The arrest of Chief Cummings by federal narcotics agents is expected later today.

According to the affidavits, Cummings, 59, under the guise of establishing a home in Mexico preparatory to his retirement a year hence, has been smuggling drugs in from Mexico on a monthly basis for more than four years.

Street prices for these drugs have totaled as much as $75,000 a month.

Cummings's personal car, which he used on his frequent trips to Mexico, is a late-model dark blue Chevrolet sedan, with plates front and back reading "Chief of Police." The car is equipped with a police radio. A rotating, flashing light similar to those used on official police cars is on the roof of Cummings's privately owned car. A high-powered Winchester rifle is slung beneath the dashboard.

It is unknown whether Cummings also wore his police uniform while going through customs.

It is known that his wife and teenage daughter frequently have made the trip with him.

Cummings has been a member of The Beach police force 19 years. Prior to his police career, he was a career non-commissioned officer in the U. S. Army.

Montgomery is the son of James Montgomery, superintendent of schools at The Beach.

According to the affidavits, town police regularly would pick up young Montgomery for "questioning."

Once alone in the office of the chief of police, the transfer of drugs for cash would take place between Montgomery and Cummings.

Montgomery states the belief these transactions were completely unknown to other police officers.

Montgomery would transfer both drugs and money in a money belt concealed beneath a loose Hawaiian shirt.

Pretending to make a purchase of drugs from Witherspoon,

Montgomery would in fact drop the drug-laden money belt in a place prearranged for Witherspoon to find it.

Although the widespread presence of illegal drugs in The Beach area was visible, the method of how the drugs came to be in the area was invisible.

An earlier drug-runner, a 19-year-old simply identified in the affidavits as "Jeff," reportedly committed suicide four years ago.

The handwritten note allegedly from Cummings was written at the time of "Jeff's" suicide. It refers to the problem of replacing "Jeff" as a drug-runner by Montgomery.

According to his own affidavit, Montgomery has been running drugs since the age of fourteen.

Originally, when it was time for another transfer, Montgomery would signal Cummings by leaving his bicycle chained to a parking meter visible through the window of the office of the chief of police. The bicycle had a distinct, purple banana seat and a high rear-view mirror.

Later, the signal that Montgomery wanted to be "picked up for questioning" so a transfer of money for drugs could take place would be his parking a flower-decorated Volkswagen minibus within sight of the police chief's office window. The vehicle is registered to Witherspoon.

Witherspoon, 38, has been living apparently undisturbed by police in a lean-to on the beach for years.

He identifies himself as a former music teacher with the Denver, Colo., public school system.

In his affidavit, Witherspoon states that he and only he has been selling the drugs supplied by Cummings in The Beach area.

Both Witherspoon and Montgomery state they had no share in the profits from the illegal drug trade. Self-attested addicts, they profited only by having their own drug needs supplied free of charge by Cummings.

They both attest that they were forced to continue in this traffic by Chief Cummings, who threatened them with evidence in his possession that they had been involved in drug-dealing.

Witherspoon had sold drugs illegally in The Beach area before becoming an agent of the police chief.

Witherspoon stated, "I was as much a prisoner of the chief of police, both by my need for drugs and by evidence he had on me, as I would have been if I were sitting in the town jail."

171

As chief of police, Cummings had refused offers of assistance from private sources to have the town's drug problems investigated by outside experts. Such a repeated offer by John Collins, chairman of the board of Collins Aviation, was repeatedly refused.

According to Collins, Cummings always insisted he was "within a few months" of breaking the case.

He made a similar insistence to the *News-Tribune* Tuesday of this week.

After handing in the originals and duplicates of both stories to the copy desk of the afternoon newspaper, Fletch spent time identifying the photographs he had ordered processed two days before and drafting captions for them. The photographs were of Roberta Sanders, Police Chief Graham Cummings (which had been in the *News-Tribune* picture files), Charles Witherspoon outside the lean-to handing a small cellophane-wrapped package of heroin to Creasey, who was not identifiable in the photograph, and of Lewis Montgomery dressed in a Hawaiian shirt standing beside the Volkswagen minibus.

He Xeroxed two copies each of the affidavits and Cummings's handwritten note and turned both copies over to the copy desk. One clear copy of each would be photographed, engraved and printed in the *News-Tribune* with his second story.

The originals of the affidavits and the handwritten note he brought back to his office and placed in an addressed envelope. He telephoned for a city messenger. Then he sealed the envelope.

It was only then that Fletch made the telephone contacts he had already reported in news stories already being printed.

"Beach Police. Please state your name and the number from which you are calling."

With his handkerchief between his mouth and the telephone receiver, Fletch said, "I want to report a body."

"Please state your name and the number from which you are calling."

"There's a body buried on the beach, of a girl—the girl Bobbi. She is buried in a sleeping bag. She's dead."

"Who is this?"

"This is not a hoax. Bobbi is buried on the beach near the sea wall. The only place along the sea wall where the sand is perpetually in the shade. Where it curves and the sidewalk overhangs. Up the beach from Fat Sam's lean-to. There is a rock from the sea wall placed over the exact spot where she is buried. Have you got that?"

"Please repeat."

"The body of Bobbi is buried on the beach, next to the sea wall not far from Fat Sam's lean-to. There is a rock placed precisely on the sand where she is buried."

"Please identify yourself. Who is this calling?"

Fletch said, "Please find Bobbi."

At seven forty-five Thursday morning, the city messenger appeared in Fletch's office. He was about twenty-five years old, wearing a black leather jacket and carrying a motorcycle helmet.

Without saying anything, Fletch handed him the envelope containing the original affidavits and the original of Cummings's handwritten note.

The messenger read the address and, without saying anything, left.

At seven-fifty, Fletch dialed a suburban number.

"Hello?"

"Good morning, Audrey. You sound as fresh as a morning glory."

"Fletcher? Is that you?"

"Sharp as a tack, too."

"Why are you calling at this hour? I'm trying to get the kids off to school."

"I just wanted to make sure you're awake and have the coffee on for Alston."

"He's had his coffee. He's just leaving for the office."

"Call him back, will you, Audrey? I need to speak to him."

"He's right here. Trying to kiss me good-bye."

"How could he, ever?"

"Fletcher, you're sweet. Here's Alston."

"Is this Alston Chambers, our distinguished district attorney?"

"Hiya, buddy. I'm not district attorney. I'm what is known as the district attorney's office. That means I just do all the work."

"I know. Audrey sounds pretty fresh for eight o'clock in the morning."

"She makes up for the coffee with morning sprightliness. I can't stand either. That's why I leave for the office so early. What's up, buddy?"

"Alston, I'm sending over to your office by messenger a couple of depositions or affidavits or whatever you legal types call them, and a signed, handwritten note. They should be in your office by the time you get there."

"Okay. What do they say?"

"They should be self-explanatory. Briefly what they say is that Graham Cummings, the chief of police at The Beach, is and has been for at least four years the source of illegal drugs in The Beach area."

"Wow. Graham Cummings? He's as clean as a hound dog's tooth."

"We thought he was as clean as a hound dog's tooth."

"I'm sorry to hear this."

"Actually, so am I."

"Has anybody arrested him yet?"

"No. That's a bit of a problem, as you can see. You'll have to arrange that."

"Right, Irwin. It will take time."

"Time?"

"A few hours. First, I have to get your depositions and copy them. Then I'll have to get in touch with federal narcotics agents, show them the depositions, and so forth. Then they'll have to send someone down there, after having gotten an arrest warrant."

"Don't be too long about it. If you miss him, he'll probably head for the Mexican border in his own car, which looks like a police car, bubble machine and all. He has a police radio in the car and a high-powered rifle. Apparently he's used it to fool Customs a lot. Anyway, it's a dark blue Chevrolet sedan, license number 706-552."

"Give me the number again."

"706-552."

174

"Okay. Sure you're right about this?"

"Yup."

"Boy. Graham Cummings. I can't believe it."

"Look, Alston, even before you pick up Cummings, there's something else I want you to do for me."

"You've already given me a morning's work."

"I know, but I want the two people who signed these affidavits to be picked up and put in protective custody."

"Right. Where are they?"

"At eleven o'clock this morning, they'll be waiting to be picked up at the beer stand at the main section of The Beach. You know, the beer stand that you can see from Shoreside Boulevard."

"I know the place."

"They'll be there waiting."

"What are their names?"

"Witherspoon and Montgomery. A couple of terrible-lookin' fellas. Witherspoon's thirty-eight; Montgomery's seventeen. Their names will be on the depositions."

"Of course."

"And Alston, be quick about this, will you? I've already got the story splashed all over the afternoon paper, and you know that comes off the presses at eleven-twenty-two."

"Ah, yes: Fletcher, the terrific journalist."

"And there is a death involved here—"

"Murder?"

"No. A fifteen-year-old girl found overdosed this morning at The Beach. Cummings could turn into a dangerous man very easily."

"Fletcher, did I ever tell you you're a great journalist?"

"No."

"Irwin Fletcher, you are. You really are. I hope the *News-Tribune* appreciates you."

"They're about to fire me."

"Nonsense."

"Something about my not wearing shoes in the office."

"Hey, old buddy Irwin, I get to see you honored tomorrow."

"What do you mean?"

"Thanks for inviting me to witness your receiving the Bronze Star."

"I didn't invite you."

"I got an invitation from the promotion department of the *News-Tribune*."

"I didn't send it."

"You must have made up the invitation list."

"I made up no invitation list."

"I'm coming anyway. All us old comrades-in-arms are very proud of you, you know. All I ever won in the marines was a disease coffee doesn't cure."

"Do you still have it?"

"No. I lost it on a toilet seat."

"At City Hall, I hope."

"Probably. I thought you picked up the Bronze Star years ago."

"I never picked it up."

"Will you pick it up tomorrow?"

"Sure," Fletch said. "Sure, sure, sure."

"I'll be there."

"You be there. Better look pretty—there will be photographers."

"I'll wear a smile. See you then, Fletch."

"See you then."

"Fletcher!"

It was nine-thirty in the morning, and Fletch was going home for the day. He had waited to see the front-page proof at nine-fifteen. It was beautiful. Both stories began above the fold, with pictures of Bobbi and Cummings. The jumps, with more pictures, would be on page three, with full reproductions of the affidavits and handwritten note and more pictures. A blockbuster. Copy editors had changed very little of his copy. A veritable one-two helluva blockbuster.

He had the key in the ignition of the MG.

"Oh, hello, Clara."

She had parked her gray Vega station wagon down the line of cars waiting to take their owners home again.

"How are you, sweetheart?"

"Fletcher, this is Thursday."

"I know."

She was leaning over his car door like a traffic officer.

"Where are you going?"

"Home."

"I haven't seen the beach-drug story yet."

"I know."

"I told you you're to have that story in by four o'clock this afternoon."

"When would you run it?"

"I don't know. I'll have to do some work on it first."

"Would you run it tomorrow?"

"I don't know. It depends on how much work we have to do on it."

"Would you run it in the Sunday paper?"

"I don't know. Frank said something about holding it for a week or two. He said he wanted to see it too. He said you had some crazy idea Graham Cummings is implicated."

"Did I say that?"

"They're friends."

"Oh."

"Is Cummings implicated?"

"His name is mentioned in the story."

"It's up to Frank and me when the story runs in the paper. It's your job to get the story on my desk by four o'clock this afternoon."

"Have I ever disappointed you yet, Clara?"

"I'm serious, Fletcher."

"Have no fear. You'll see the story this afternoon."

"You're sure?"

"Clara: I'm absolutely sure. This afternoon you'll see the drug-beach story."

"I'd better."

"You will."

"And you'd better plan on being in the marine commandant's office at ten o'clock tomorrow morning."

"Don't worry about that, either."

"Okay. Your job is on the line."

"I'd hate to lose it," Fletch said. "You know how I love working with you."

Fletch turned the ignition key.

"Fletch, I'll see you by four o'clock at the latest."

"You'll see the story by four o'clock," Fletch said. "Maybe even a little earlier."

30

Fletch spent most of Thursday alone in his apartment.

He ate.

He slept.

He destroyed the Stanwyk tape.

He typed a letter to John Collins. He typed an original and a single carbon copy of the letter. And threw the original of the letter away. The copy he placed folded in the inside pocket of his suit jacket.

He emptied the wastebaskets.

At eleven-thirty, the phone began ringing persistently. He knew it was Clara Snow and/or Frank Jaffe or any one of several other *News-Tribune* executives who characteristically became excited, one way or the other, in pleasure if they were real professionals, in anger if they were not, when a staff member had snuck a genuine, unadulterated piece of journalism over on them. In all newspapers Fletch had seen there was always a hard core of genuinely professional working staff which made it possible to commit genuine journalism occasionally, regardless of the incompetence among the executive staff. The afternoon newspaper was on the streets. The excited callers apparently went out to lunch at one o'clock. The phone did not begin ringing relentlessly again until two-thirty.

At three o'clock the lobby doorbell rang.

Fletch pressed the buzzer to unlock the downstairs lobby door and waited.

In a moment his own apartment doorbell rang.

He opened the door to Joan Collins Stanwyk.

"Good afternoon, Mr. Fletcher."

"Good afternoon, Mrs. Stanwyk."

"Fletcher, as I said, is a name I can remember."

"You know who I am?"

"Thank you, I do."

"Won't you come in?"

She entered and sat on the divan.

"May I offer you a drink?"

"No, thank you, Mr. Fletcher. But you may offer me an explanation."

"Ah?"

Fletch remained standing, taking a step this way, a step that. In the eleventh hour, his cover had been blown.

"Mr. Fletcher, why are you investigating my husband? Or is it I you are investigating?"

"Neither of you," Fletch said.

Also, he found this Mr. and Mrs. business a bit cumbersome between two people who had made love both Polish and Rumanian style only two days before.

"What makes you think I am investigating you?"

"Mr. Fletcher, I have been born, bred and educated to do a job, as I gather you have, because clearly you are very good at your job. My job is to support and protect my father and my husband. And I'm rather good at it."

"In fact, protect Collins Aviation."

"And its investors, and the people it employs, et cetera."

"I see."

"One can't have this subtle job for as many years as I've had it without developing certain subtle instincts. At lunch at the Racquets Club Saturday, when you and I first met, after a while my intuition told me I was being questioned. For the life of me, I could not figure what I was being questioned about. So I took your picture."

Without looking at it, she transferred it from her purse to the coffee table. It was a three-quarter Polaroid shot of Fletch in a tennis shirt in the Racquets Club pavilion.

"While you were getting another chair for the table, after my father joined us. I turned your picture over to Collins plant security Monday morning. It was just this morning I received their report. You are I. M. Fletcher of the *News-Tribune*. Your identity was confirmed by a city police detective named Lupo, and has since been confirmed again by the newspaper itself."

Fletch said, "Wow."

Prowling the room, watching her, Fletch had the sudden, irrational desire to marry Joan Collins Stanwyk.

"Now, Mr. Fletcher, when a newspaper reporter ingratiates himself into one's acquaintanceship—in this case, I might even say into one's intimacy—under a false name, an entirely false identity, one can safely assume one is being investigated."

"Right."

"But you say you're not investigating us."

"Right. Your father. John Collins. I wanted some information from him."

"Your phone is ringing."

"I know."

"Seeing you apparently don't answer your phone, may I ask what information you wanted from my father?"

"Whether or not he had ever offered to subsidize a private investigation of the source of drugs at The Beach, and whether or not the chief of police, Graham Cummings, had ever refused his help."

"Of what conceivable use could that piece of information be to you?"

"I've already printed it. Have you seen this afternoon's *News-Tribune?*"

"No, I haven't."

"I busted your local drug story wide open. Cummings is the source of the drugs. In one paragraph, I believe paragraph thirty-four, I report your father's offers. If I had asked your father officially or directly, he would never have told me, for fear it would reflect upon the chief of police, never dreaming it is the chief himself who is guilty."

180

"How very interesting. You go to that much effort for one paragraph?"

"You should see the efforts I go to sometimes for paragraphs I don't even write."

"But I have the distinct impression it was my father who first brought up the topic of drugs, not you."

"You can't be sure, can you?"

"No, I can't. Have you ever known my husband?"

"No."

"How were you so able to convince us that you had known him and known him well? That you had even attended the wedding?"

'Newspaper research. Plain old homework."

"But you even knew that he had buzzed a house in San Antonio, Texas, years ago. We didn't know that."

"How do you know it's true?"

"I asked him."

"You asked him?"

"Yes. He was embarrassed, but he didn't deny it."

"That's funny."

"How did you know it?"

"It's on his police record. That and a six-month-old unpaid parking ticket in Los Angeles."

"And why would you look up his police record if you are not investigating him?"

"I wanted to have some detail of information to convince you that I knew him."

"I'm having great difficulty believing you would go to such lengths for one, unimportant paragraph in a news story which really doesn't concern us."

"Believe me. I'm absolutely honest."

"Your phone is ringing."

"I know."

Joan Collins Stanwyk said, "In trying to focus upon what your line of questioning was, if there was one, I believed it had to do with your curiosity concerning my husband's health."

"How is he, by the way?"

"Fine, as far as I know. But your questions concerned his health. You even pinned down the name and address of his insurance agent. And I think—I'm not sure—you even mentioned the name of the family doctor."

Standing in the room, looking at Joan Collins Stanwyk sitting with dignity on the divan, Fletch was full of joy. She was wonderful. A woman who penetrated his sense of play, could reconstruct it, come close to understanding his moves, he should love forever.

And in a few hours he was scheduled to murder her husband—at the request of the man himself.

He said, "I have no idea what you're talking about. All that was idle chatter."

"Secondly, you directed a great many questions to me, and virtually none to my father. With him, again the question of Alan's health came up."

"What else is there to talk about? The weather. When one has nothing to talk about, one talks about either the weather or someone's health."

"Do you know anything about my husband's health that I don't know?"

"Honestly, I don't."

"How did you get into the Racquets Club, Mr. Fletcher?"

"I bought a pair of tennis shorts and said I was a guest of the Underwoods."

"Do you know the Underwoods?"

"No. I read the name from a locker."

"I will have to reimburse them for any expenses you incurred."

"It shouldn't be much. Two screwdrivers."

"Nevertheless, I will reimburse them for two screwdrivers. You don't even play tennis?"

"I play with people. Somehow I don't like the word 'court.' Not even 'tennis court.' Once playing with people gets close to a court, things are apt to get boring."

"Is that because in a court there are rules?"

"It may be."

"Your phone is ringing."

182

"I know."

"Was our going to bed together Tuesday night a part of your investigation?"

"No. That was on my own time."

"I sincerely hope so."

"Do you intend to tell your husband about I. M. Fletcher of the *News-Tribune?*"

"Mr. Fletcher, how can I?"

Fletch finally sat on the divan.

"People call me Fletch."

"I have a committee meeting at the Racquets Club. It's Thursday evening. I have to pick up Julie. The servants are away."

"There's always time."

"Fletch. Your phone is ringing."

"I know."

At six o'clock the apartment doorbell rang again. Fletch was alone. He had showered and put on a suit. The downstairs lobby bell had not rung.

At the door were two very young, very scrubbed men who were very obviously police detectives.

"Mr. I. M. Fletcher?"

Fletch said, "I'm sorry, Mr. Fletcher isn't in. I'm his attorney, Mr. Gillett of Gillett, Worsham and O'Brien. Is there anything I can do for you?"

"You're his attorney?"

"That's right."

"We have a warrant for the arrest of I. M. Fletcher of this address to face charges of criminal fraud."

"Yes, I know. I've advised Mr. Fletcher on this matter."

"Where is he?"

"Well, gentlemen, I'll tell you. The man is as guilty as sin. He's spending this afternoon and evening trying to wind up personal business. You do understand."

"This isn't the first time we've come here trying to locate him."

"Never fear. I promise you I will bring Mr. Fletcher to the main police station tomorrow morning at ten o'clock, where he will surrender himself. He just needs tonight to iron things out for himself."

"What's tomorrow, Friday?"

"He will surrender himself Friday morning at ten o'clock."

"In your recognizance?"

Fletch smiled patronizingly, as attorneys always do when police officers use large legal terms.

"In my recognizance."

"What's your name again?"

"Mr. Gillett, of Gillett, Worsham and O'Brien. My firm is here in the city."

Fletch watched one of the policemen write in a notebook: "Gillett—Gillett, Worsham and O'Brien."

The other policeman said, "You do realize, sir, that if you do not surrender I. M. Fletcher tomorrow morning, you too will be liable for criminal arrest?"

"Of course I realize it," Fletch said. "After all, I am a member of the California bar and an officer of the court."

"Okay."

Fletch said, "Wait a minute, officers, I'll walk out with you. Which way is the elevator?"

"This way, sir."

"Oh, thank you."

Fletch then drove to the Stanwyk residence on Berman Street.

31

It was eight-thirty Thursday night.

Dressed in a full business suit, shirt and tie, Fletch opened the french windows to the library of the Stanwyk house and entered.

Alan Stanwyk, smoking a cigarette, was waiting in a leather chair the other side of the desk. He had bleached his hair blond.

"Good evening, Mr. Stanwyk. I.M. Fletcher, of the *News-Tribune*. May I use your phone?"

Stanwyk's left knee jerked.

Fletch picked up the phone and dialed.

"This won't take a minute."

He took the folded copy of the letter from his inside suit jacket and handed it across to Stanwyk while listening for the phone to be answered.

"Here, you can read this while you're waiting. Copies go to those people indicated at midnight, unless I make a coded phone call saying not to send them. Hello, Audrey? Fletcher. Is Alston there?"

Stanwyk had leaned forward across the desk and taken the letter.

Mr. John Collins,
Chairman of the Board,
Collins Aviation
#1 Collins Plaza
Greenway, California

Dear Sir:

Alan Stanwyk murdered me tonight.

The charred remains are mine, regardless of the evidence of the Colgate ring and the gold cigarette lighter identified as belonging to Stanwyk.

Stanwyk boarded a plane chartered from Command Air Charter Service in my name for Rio de Janeiro, where he intends to establish residence under my name with the aid of my passport.

For the purpose, he has bleached his hair blond. He stole the bleach from the apartment of his mistress, Sandra Faulkner, 15641B Putnam Street, Monday night.

With Stanwyk in Rio de Janeiro are a Mrs. Sally Ann Cushing Cavanaugh, and son, William, of Nonheagan, Pennsylvania. Stanwyk has been visiting Mrs. Cavanaugh in Nonheagan on the average of every six weeks for at least four years. This can be confirmed by a pilot called "Bucky" in your employ. Mrs. Cavanaugh was recently divorced from her husband.

185

Also with Stanwyk in Rio are three million dollars in cash. This money is the result of sales of stock by broker William Carmichael, who believed the cash was required as down payment for a ranch in Nevada being bought through Swarthout Nevada Realty.

Sincerely,

I.M. Fletcher

cc: Joan Collins Stanwyk
William Carmichael
Burt Eberhart
Alston Chambers

"Hello, Alston? Fletch."

"The world's greatest journalist?"

"The very same. How did everything go?"

"Terrific. The affidavits are fine. That handwritten note from Cummings is beyond belief. We picked up your little birds, Witherspoon and Montgomery, and they've been singing all afternoon."

"Are they all right?"

"We have them in protective custody under assumed names in a hospital far, far away from here."

"That's great." Stanwyk was reading the letter a second or a third time. "You do nice work, Alston."

"You made quite a splash in the afternoon paper, Irwin. This case is the biggest local sensation of the year."

"Would you believe I never saw it?"

"You ought to read your own newspaper."

"I can't afford to buy it on a reporter's salary."

Beside the desk were neatly placed two matching attaché cases.

"There is one thing more, Alston."

"What's that, old buddy?"

"You haven't arrested the chief of police yet. It's only a small matter, I know, a minor detail, but the son of a bitch just followed me in his car."

"Where are you?"

"He followed me from The Beach to The Hills."

"Is he still with you?"

186

"I guess so. It was his car all right. The private car that looks like a police car."

"Fletch; there are federal narcotics agents waiting for him both at the police station and at his home. They've been there for hours."

"Couldn't they get up off their tails and go out into the streets and find the bastard?"

"They don't know the area. You can't outfox a police chief in his own town. If worse comes to worst, we'll catch him at the border."

"Terrific. What about me?"

"Just shout out the window at him. Tell him to go home."

"Thanks."

"Don't worry about a thing, Fletch. They'll get him. And I'll see you in the marine commandant's office at ten in the morning. Be sure to shine your shoes."

"Pick the son of a bitch up."

"We will, we will. Good night, Fletch."

Stanwyk was sitting in the red leather chair with the copy of the letter in his hand. On the table beside him were his Colgate ring and the gold cigarette lighter.

He was staring calmly at Fletch.

"I guess you don't get to do what you want to do," Fletch said.

"I guess not."

"The thing that tipped me off was something your wife said the other night when we were in bed together."

Fletch sat at the desk.

"She said you and I have identical bone structures. We look nothing alike. You're dark, I'm blond. You weigh ten or twelve pounds more than I do. But our bone structures are alike. That's why you picked me from all the drifters on the beach.

"Your plan was to murder me somehow—probably, as you've boxed, with your hands—knock me unconscious, strangle me. Then fake a car accident. Only as a burned corpse could I pass for you. I would be wearing your clothes, your shoes and your ring and carrying your cigarette lighter, burned to death in your car. No one would question it."

187

"Quite right."

"Are there three million dollars in those attaché cases?"

"Yes."

"You needed a chartered plane to avoid an airlines baggage check. Carrying three million dollars in cash on a commercial airliner would be noticed."

Stanwyk said, "Remarkable. At no point during this last week have I had the slightest sensation of being investigated."

"You thoroughly expected to murder me tonight."

"Yes."

"After investigating you off and on all week, I must say that puzzles me. Generally speaking, you're a decent man. How did you intend to justify murder to yourself?"

"You mean, morally justify it?"

"Yes."

"I have the right to kill anyone who has agreed to murder me, under any circumstances. Don't you agree?"

"I see."

"Putting it most simply, Mr. Fletcher, I wanted out."

"Many people do."

"And now, Mr. Fletcher, what do we do?"

"Do?"

Stanwyk was standing, hands behind his back, facing the french windows. He could not see through the transparent curtain from the lighted room into the dark outdoors. The man was thinking furiously.

He said, "I see I've put myself into a rather difficult position."

"Oh?"

"I can see you are probably going to do precisely as I asked: you are going to murder me."

Fletch said nothing.

"I have arranged the perfect crime against myself. We are alone. No wife, no servants. There is nothing to connect you and me. And I imagine that in your investigating me this week, you were very careful not to connect you and me."

"I was."

"I have guaranteed your escape. Only you take the charter flight rather than the TWA flight."

"Right."

"The difference is that there are three million dollars at your feet, rather than fifty thousand. Surely that's enough to make any man commit murder."

In the air-conditioned room, Stanwyk's face was gleaming with perspiration.

"The only thing you don't know is that the gun in the desk drawer is empty."

"I do know that. I checked it early this morning. You're right. The servants always do leave the french windows unlocked."

"Therefore, I would guess you have brought your own implement of death, your own gun, and you do mean to kill me. Am I right?"

Fletch opened the top right-hand drawer of the desk.

"No. I just brought a full clip for this gun."

While Stanwyk watched from the windows, Fletch picked up the gun in one hand; with the other hand he took a full .38 caliber clip from his pocket.

"You pointed out to me the benefit of using your gun."

He removed the blank clip from the gun and inserted the full clip.

Stanwyk said, "You're not wearing gloves."

"Nothing a quick dust with a handkerchief can't fix."

"Christ."

"You've not only arranged your own murder perfectly, you've even given me a moral justification for it. You say you have the right to kill anyone who has planned to murder you. Isn't that what you said?"

"Yes."

"So why shouldn't I murder you, Stanwyk?"

"I don't know."

"For three million dollars rather than fifty grand. Alone with you in your house, as you nicely arranged. Using your gun. Nothing to connect us to each other. With a prearranged, guaranteed escape. And a moral justification, provided by yourself. I'm sure I can make it look exactly like the usual burglary-murder you originally described."

"You're playing with me, Fletcher."

"Yes, I am."

"I repeat my original request: if you're going to murder me, do it quickly and painlessly."

"Either the head or the heart. Is that what you said?"

"Have some decency."

"I'm not going to murder you."

Fletch put the gun in his pocket.

"I'm not going to murder you, rob you, blackmail you or expose you. I can't think of a single reason why I should do any of those things. You'll just have to find another way to establish life with Sally Ann Cushing Cavanaugh.

"Good night, Mr. Stanwyk."

"Fletcher."

Fletch turned at the door to the front hall.

"If you're not going to do any of those things, why did you go to all this effort?"

Fletch said, "Beats tennis."

The room shattered.

The light curtains over the french windows billowed forward as if caught by a sudden puff of wind. There were two explosive cracks. Glass tinkled.

The front of Stanwyk's chest blew open. His arms and chin jerked up. Without his having stepped, his body raised so that the toes of his black shoes pointed downward.

From that position, he fell to the floor, his knees thudding against the rug. Stanwyk rolled to his right shoulder and landed on his back.

"Christ."

Fletch knelt beside him.

"You've been shot."

"Who? Who shot me?"

"Would you believe the chief of police?"

"Why?"

"He thought you were me. We have the same bone structure, and you bleached your hair blond."

190

"He was trying to kill you?"

"Stanwyk, you've killed yourself."

"Am I dying?"

"I don't know how you're breathing now."

"Fletcher. Nail the bastard. Use the money. Nail the bastard."

"I already have."

"Nail the bastard."

"Okay."

With his handkerchief, Fletch removed his fingerprints from the gun and the gun clip. He exchanged clips and returned the gun to the drawer. He dusted the handle to the desk drawer, the telephone, the desk itself, and the outside handle to the french window.

Stanwyk was dead on the rug.

The copy of the letter he had addressed to John Collins was on the table beside the leather chair. Fletch folded it and put it back in his pocket.

Then, taking the two attaché cases, Fletch carefully let himself out of the house.

His MG was parked in front.

32

"Ah, Mr. Fletcher."

"I just have to make a phone call. It will take me about twenty minutes."

"Then we'll take your luggage aboard, sir. Just the suitcase and these two attaché cases?"

"Yes. Is there a phone?"

"Use the phone in the office, sir. Just dial nine and then your number. We'll be ready for departure when you are."

Fletch dialed nine and then the recorder number of the *News-Tribune*. He sat at the wooden desk. The door with the opaque glass to the Command Air Charter Service lobby was closed.

191

"This is Fletcher. Who's catching?"

"It's me, Mr. Fletcher. Bobby Evans."

"How are ya doin', Bobby?"

"Helluva story this morning, Mr. Fletcher."

"Thanks for reading the *News-Tribune*. Look, Bobby, no one's expecting this one. Will you square with the desk for me? I'm in sort of a hurry."

"More of the same?"

"Sort of. I want to get out of here. Another thing, Bobby. I haven't written this story yet. I'm just dictating off the top of my head."

"Okay, Mr. Fletcher."

"So if you hear anything wrong, grab it right away. I can't go back over it."

"Okay."

"Another thing. When I get done with the story I'd like you to take a little note to Clara Snow."

"That isn't usually done."

"I know, but I won't be in the office in the morning. I'm going to have to miss an appointment."

"Okay."

"Is the blower on?"

"Go ahead, Mr. Fletcher."

"Friday A.M. parenthesis fp unparenthesis Stanwyk Murder Fletcher.

"Alan Stanwyk, one l, a, w-y-k, thirty-three-year-old executive vice president of Collins Aviation, was shot and killed in the library of his home on Berman Street, The Hills, last night."

"Wow."

"Chief of Police of The Beach, Graham Cummings, is being questioned about the murder."

"Wow, wow. Mr. Fletcher, there hasn't been anything on the police radios about this yet."

"I know. Paragraph three. Police estimate the time of the murder at nine-thirty.

"Paragraph. The body was discovered by the victim's wife, Joan Collins Stanwyk, upon her return from a committee meeting at the Racquets Club at eleven o'clock."

"Mr. Fletcher?"

"What?"

"You said the body was discovered at eleven o'clock."

"I know."

"It's only ten-fifteen now, Mr. Fletcher."

"I know.

"Paragraph. According to a police spokesman, Stanwyk was shot twice in the back through a window by a high-powered rifle. Death was instantaneous.

"Paragraph. Ballistic tests are being made this morning to determine if the murder weapon is the same as the high-powered Winchester rifle Cummings kept slung from the dashboard of his private car.

"Paragraph. Cummings, fifty-nine, was named in a *News-Tribune* report yesterday afternoon concerning the source of illegal drugs in The Beach area.

"Paragraph. Evidence presented to the district attorney's office yesterday morning by the *News-Tribune* included affidavits signed by a self-admitted drug peddler, Charles Witherspoon, thirty-eight, alias Vatsyayana, alias Fat Sam, and a self-admitted drug runner, Lewis Montgomery, seventeen, alias Gummy two *m*'s, *y*. Other evidence was a note written in Cummings's hand to Witherspoon concerning the drug traffic.

"Paragraph. Both affidavits named Cummings as the principal source of illegal drugs at The Beach.

"Paragraph. Beach police yesterday discovered the body of a fifteen-year-old girl, Roberta quote Bobbi unquote Sanders no *u,* buried in a sleeping bag in the sand near Witherspoon's lean-to. She died of a drug overdose.

"Paragraph. Warrants for the arrest of Cummings were issued yesterday afternoon.

"Paragraph. Cummings had not been taken into police custody at the time of the murder at the Stanwyk residence.

"Paragraph. This reporter saw Cummings alone in his private car in the area of the Stanwyk residence at eight-thirty last night, and reported seeing him by telephone to assistant district attorney Alston Chambers one *l.*

"Paragraph. There is no evidence that Stanwyk and Cummings knew each other, although Stanwyk's father-in-law, John Collins, president and chairman of the board of Collins Aviation, several times has pressured Cummings as chief of police to discover and destroy the source of illegal drugs in The Beach area.

"Paragraph. Collins lives within walking distance of the Stanwyk house.

"Paragraph. Reportedly, Joan Stanwyk expressed surprise at finding the victim's hair bleached blond. Her husband had dark hair and had not been known previously to bleach it.

"Paragraph. This morning the victim's widow is under heavy sedation in the care of family physician, Dr. Joseph Devlin of the Medical Center.

"Paragraph. Insurance agent Burt Eberhart has confirmed that Stanwyk's life was insured for three million dollars. The extraordinary amount of insurance coverage is explained by Eberhart as being related to Stanwyk's frequent piloting of experimental aircraft.

"Paragraph. Stanwyk, a native of Nonheagan, Pennsylvania, *N-o-n-h-e-a-g-a-n,* was a graduate of Colgate College and the Wharton School of Business. As a captain in the Air Force, he flew twenty-four missions over Indochina. Shot down twice, Stanwyk was a recipient of a Purple Heart.

"Paragraph. He served as treasurer of the Racquets, plural, Club. He was a member of the Urban Club.

"Paragraph. Besides his wife, Stanwyk leaves a daughter, Julia, five, and his parents, Marvin and Helen Stanwyk, of Nonheagan, Pennsylvania. Thirty. You got that?"

"Mr. Fletcher?"

"Yes?"

"You mean this all happened last night?"

"No. Tonight."

"But how can you report a murder and even name the murderer when the body hasn't even been found yet?"

"Just make sure everything is spelled right, will you, Bobby?"

"But you say the body is discovered at eleven o'clock and it's only ten-thirty."

"Yeah. I want to make first edition."

"But, Mr. Fletcher, it hasn't happened yet."

"You're right, Bobby. Advise the desk that photographers should be sent out to the Stanwyk residence, but ask them please to wait until the widow gets home and discovers the body. It's only decent. For first edition they can use pictures from the library."

"Okay, Mr. Fletcher."

"One other thing, Bobby. I think I forgot to put in Mrs. Stanwyk's age. She's twenty-nine."

"Right."

"Please insert it."

"What about the note you want me to take to Clara Snow?"

"Oh, yeah. Dear Clara. Leaving; area too hot tonight. Frank says you're lousy in bed, too. Love, Fletch."

"Really?"

"Really."

"You want me to write that?"

"I sure do. Just don't indicate you were the one who typed it. Good night, Bobby."

"Anytime you're ready, Mr. Fletcher."

"I'm ready."

"A woman and child are waiting in the lobby. For some reason she won't say for whom they are waiting. Are they waiting for you? We haven't put their baggage aboard . . ."

"No, they're not waiting for me."

"The boy has mentioned an 'Uncle Alan.' We have no other flights tonight."

Sally Ann Cushing Cavanaugh and son William were standing in the lobby with five pieces of baggage at their feet. The boy was looking through the opened office door at Fletch.

She looked like a wonderful person. A real person. The sort Marvin Stanwyk would like, as would his son. The sort Alan Stanwyk would never have forgotten and always would have needed. The sort of girl who could make a boy give up boxing and a man give up flying. She looked like home.

195

The boy's stare was level and curious.

"No," Fletch said. "They're not waiting for me."

On the chartered jet was a heavy leather swivel lounge chair into which Fletch buckled himself.

His suitcase and the two attaché cases he had seen stored behind a drop-curtain in the stern.

With a minimum of fuss, and a maximum of silence, the Lear jet lifted into the sky.

It was eleven o'clock Thursday night.

"Would you like a drink and something to eat, Mr. Fletcher?"

"Yes."

The steward wore a white coat and black bowtie.

"Perhaps a drink first?"

"Yes. What's aboard?"

"Beefeater gin. Wild Turkey bourbon. Chivas Regal scotch—"

"What is there to eat?"

"We've stocked both a capon dinner for you, and club steak."

At ten o'clock in the morning, he would not have to be standing in court facing contempt charges for failing to pay his first wife, Barbara, eight thousand four hundred and twelve dollars in alimony.

"That sounds very nice."

"Yes, sir."

"Vermouth?"

"Yes, sir."

"Lemon?"

"Yes, sir."

At ten o'clock the next morning, he would not be standing in court facing contempt charges for failing to pay his second wife, Linda, three thousand four hundred twenty-nine dollars and forty-seven cents in alimony.

"Would you like a martini, sir?"

"I would like two martinis."

"Yes, sir."

"Each made fresh."

At ten o'clock the next morning, he would not be standing in the marine commandant's office, with photographers' flashbulbs popping, having the old tale told again, receiving the Bronze Star.

"Of course, sir."

"Then I would like the capon. Do we have an appropriate wine?"

"Yes, sir. A selection of three."

"All for the capon?"

"Yes, sir."

At ten o'clock the next morning, he would not be standing before the booking desk at the main police station being charged with criminal fraud.

"After the capon, I would like two scotches."

"Yes, sir."

"Cracked ice."

"Of course, sir."

At ten o'clock the next morning, his two ex-wives, Barbara and Linda, each having given up her own apartment, would be moving into his apartment, to live with each other.

"Then I would like the club steak. Fairly rare."

"As another supper, sir?"

"Yes."

"I see, sir."

And shortly after ten o'clock in the morning, a warrant for the arrest of Gillett, of Gillett, Worsham and O'Brien, would be issued, for aiding a fugitive escape justice.

"With the steak I would like an ale. Do we have ale on board?"

"Yes, sir."

"That's fine. It should be very cold."

"Yes, sir."

Fletch was flying over Mexico with three million dollars in tens and twenties in two attaché cases.

"Would you like your first martini now, sir?"

"We'd better start sometime. We're only going as far as Rio."

197

CONFESS, FLETCH

The flight from Rome had been pleasant enough, even if the business he was on wasn't exactly. Fletch's Italian fiancée's father had been kidnapped and presumably murdered, and Fletch is on the trail of a stolen art collection that is her only patrimony. But when he arrives in his apartment to find a dead body, things start to get complicated. Inspector Flynn found him a little glib for someone who seemed to be the only likely suspect in a homicide case. With the police on his tail, Fletch makes himself at home in Boston, breaking into a private art gallery, "entertaining" his future mother-in-law, and visiting with the good Inspector Flynn.

Crime Fiction/0-375-71348-4

FLETCH'S FORTUNE

Fletch hasn't been a practicing journalist for years, although people remember him and he still has a few contacts. Enjoying himself on the French Riviera, developing a killer tan, and sleeping with the neighbor's wife, Fletch is feeling pretty flush. But when agents Eggers and Fabens show up with a little more information about Fletch than he is comfortable with and an invitation to the American Journalism Alliance, he soon finds himself enlisted as a spy among his peers. But before he can even set up his surveillance, there's a murder. And almost everybody's a suspect, because a lot of people were employed by Walter March, and most of them had a reason to hate him.

Crime Fiction/0-375-71355-7

FLETCH WON

As a fledgling reporter, Fletch is doing more flailing than anything else. That and floating around from department to department trying to figure out where he fits in. His editor's got him pegged for the society pages, but the kind of society Fletch gets involved with is anything but polite. His first big interview, a millionaire lawyer with a crooked streak and an itch to give away some of his ill-gotten gains, ends up dead in the *News-Tribune*'s parking lot before Fletch can ask question number one. So Fletch ends up going after the murderer instead. At the same time, he's supposed to be covering (or maybe uncovering) a health spa that caters to all its clients' needs, and gets hired as a *very* personal trainer.

Crime Fiction/0-375-71352-2

FLETCH AND THE WIDOW BRADLEY

When Fletch calls in to the *News-Tribune*, he discovers that he might just be out of a job. If Tom Bradley, the chairman of Wagnall-Phipps and one of Fletch's principal sources—and not incidentally, the source of his paper's embarrassment—is dead, who's been signing his name to company documents, and why doesn't the company treasurer seem to know? If he's alive, how come his widow, Enid, has Tom's ashes on the mantel? Fletch may have more questions than answers on his hands, but he knows he's a pretty good reporter, and if he's going to get his reputation back, not to mention his job, he's going to have to get to the bottom of more than one mystery.

Crime Fiction/0-375-71351-4

FLETCH, TOO

Fletch is finally getting hitched. It's a small affair, just a few friends, the bride's parents, the groom's mother, and—just maybe—his father. Except Fletch has never met his father. But somebody delivered a letter from Fletch senior that contained an invitation to visit him in Nairobi for the honeymoon, along with a pair of plane tickets. No sooner does the couple land in Africa than the search for Fletch's father begins. There's a murder at the airport, reports of the old man's incarceration, and the hospitality (and evasiveness) offered by Pop's best friend, who flies them across the continent, just a step or two behind—or maybe ahead of—the old rascal.

Crime Fiction/0-375-71353-0

CARIOCA FLETCH

Fletch's trip to Brazil wasn't exactly planned. But he has plenty of money, thanks to a little arrangement made stateside. And it took him no time to hook up with the luscious Laura Soares. Fletch is beginning to relax, just a little. But between the American widow who seems to be following Fletch and the Brazilian widow who's convinced that Fletch is her long-dead husband, Fletch suddenly doesn't have much time to enjoy the present. A thirty-year-old unsolved murder, a more recent suicide, and an inconvenient heart attack—somehow Fletch is connected to all of them, and one of those connections might just shorten his own life.

Crime Fiction/0-375-71347-6

VINTAGE CRIME/BLACK LIZARD
Available at your local bookstore, or call toll-free to order:
1-800-793-2665 (credit cards only).